FAMILY TREASURES
AND OTHER
BEDTIME STORIES

Compiled and edited by
ROSALIND PRICE
&
WALTER McVITTY

Illustrated by
RON BROOKS

ALTERNATIVE TITLE:
MACQUARIE BEDTIME STORY BOOK

HAMISH HAMILTON · LONDON

Hamish Hamilton Ltd
Published by the Penguin Group
27 Wrights Lane, London W8 5TZ, England
Viking Penguin, A Division of Penguin Books USA
375 Hudson St, New York, New York 10014, USA
Penguin Books Australia Ltd, Ringwood, Victoria, Australia
Penguin Books Canada Limited, 2801 John Street, Markham, Ontario, Canada L3R 1B4
Penguin Books (N.Z.) Ltd, 182–190 Wairau Road, Auckland 10, New Zealand

Penguin Books Ltd, Registered Offices: Harmondsworth, Middlesex, England

First published in Great Britain 1990 by Hamish Hamilton Ltd
First published in Australia by The Macquarie Library Pty Ltd, 1987
Published by Penguin Books Australia, 1990
10 9 8 7 6 5 4 3 2 1

Designed by Ron Brooks
Produced for the Publisher by P.I.X.E.L. Publishing
Offset from The Macquarie Library edition
Made and printed in Hong Kong

ISBN 0-241-12996-6

Contents

Introduction

The regular sharing of stories is an experience no child or adult should miss. There can be few better ways of ending the day than by reading a bedtime story in a relaxed, secure and loving environment. The pleasure is not only in the story itself, but in the physical and emotional closeness that grows between people who explore the magical world of fiction together in this way. For a child, such experiences will be among the most comforting, precious and long-lasting of a lifetime. And the same can be true for adults.

Many children arrive at school already able to read. These children, and those who learn to read with the greatest ease and enjoyment, are most likely to be those who come from homes where books are familiar, valued, everyday objects. These children are used to seeing others – brothers, sisters, parents – reading books as a matter of everyday custom. But more important is the fact that they have been read to regularly. As a result they have learnt that books open doors to vivid worlds of imagination, excitement, beauty and delight. Long before starting school they have discovered how books work, and they are eager to use them.

The editors have tried to cater for a range of tastes and interests as well as ages. Although there is a pattern in the arrangement, we have made no attempt to grade material according to difficulty because we feel it is better for readers to dip into the collection to find things that will suit their particular needs. A good children's story will always find its own time and level, just as all literature does.

If in doubt about what to read to a particular child, follow your own judgement. Start with something that appeals to you, and see if the child responds. If not, try something else. Don't labour a story that fails to catch the imagination; leave it for another time. You'll soon find out what works and what doesn't.

We hope that readers of this collection will find in it as much enjoyment as the authors have had in the writing, and the editors and illustrator have had in putting it all together, and that it will be dipped into for pleasure for years – perhaps generations – to come.

Rosalind Price and Walter McVitty

To Margaret, Sam and Adelaide.
To Paul, Alexander and Celia.
To Jennie and Sarah.

Morris Lurie

THE STORY OF JOSHUA, WHO JUMPED

THIS is the story of Joshua, who jumped.

Jumped like a rabbit. Jumped like a jack-in-the-box.

Jumped like a jumping kangaroo.

'Goodness me,' said his father. 'What a bouncy little fellow.'

This was when Joshua was still very small. He was still just a baby, in fact, only about six months old. But there he was, standing up in his cot, holding on to the rails with his tiny hands as firmly as he could.

His blue eyes bright and his cheeks rosy red.

And not only standing, but jumping.

Over and over.

Again and again.

'Isn't he strong?' said Joshua's father proudly.

'Doesn't he look wonderful?' said Joshua's mother, beaming.

Jump, jump, jump, went Joshua in his cot.

And his parents stood there together, hand in hand, smiling down at their jumping son.

11

Joshua learnt to crawl, of course, the way all babies do.

And then he learnt to walk, holding on to things very carefully, the way all babies do.

But the minute he learnt to walk without holding on to things, Joshua did something different.

Quite different.

Joshua stopped walking.

He forgot all about walking.

He jumped instead.

Joshua jumped everywhere.

He jumped along the passage.

He jumped into the kitchen.

He jumped around the garden, under the fruit trees, round and round the lawn.

'You don't think he's swallowed a frog?' Joshua's father smiled.

'Or a bouncy rubber ball?' Joshua's mother laughed.

Jump, jump, jump, went Joshua in the garden.

Around the lemon tree.

Under the plum tree.

Past the flowers and the bushes and the next-door hedge.

And his parents stood there together, hand in hand, laughing to see their jumping son.

Joshua jumped everywhere.

He jumped around the supermarket, when his mother took him shopping.

He jumped at the dry-cleaner's.

12   He jumped at the butcher's.

'Hmm, there's a jumpy lad,' said the butcher. 'Been feeding him lots of spring lamb, have you?'

Joshua's mother laughed.

'No, he's always been a jumper,' she said. 'It's just the way he is. A dozen sausages, please.'

When Joshua turned four, his mother took him to kindergarten. The teacher's name there was Miss Prime.

Joshua jumped up and down while he was being introduced.

'Oh, how nice!' said Miss Prime. 'I like having a chap in the class who jumps. Keeps us all on our toes! Come along, Joshua. Let's jump into some finger-painting first. And then we'll jump outside and play.'

Joshua had a wonderful time at kindergarten.

Jumping in and out of the sandpit.

On and off the swings.

He even jumped when he did his finger-paintings, and what lovely jumping pictures they were.

And then Joshua turned five and started school. That's when the trouble began.

Joshua jumped into the classroom.

It was his very first day.

His teacher's name there was Miss Stern.

And when she saw Joshua jumping in, her eyes practically jumped right out of her head.

'What?' she cried. 'Jumping? Jumping is no way to come into a class!'

Joshua looked puzzled.

'But I've always jumped,' he said. 'I've always been a jumper, from the earliest I remember.'

'Oh, how outrageous!' cried Miss Stern. 'How dare you! I've never heard such preposterous nonsense! Well, I'll show you what jumping is! You can jump into that corner over there straight away!' She pointed with a long, mean, bony finger. 'And when you get there, don't you dare move a single centimetre!'

'Yes, Miss Stern,' said Joshua.

So Joshua stood in the corner as still as still could be.

Slowly a minute dragged past.

The second minute seemed even slower.

The third was worse.

Joshua felt miserable.

He had never felt so awful in his whole life.

It was absolutely terrible to have to stand like this.

It was torture.

And before he knew what he was doing, Joshua began to bounce up and down.

Little bounces at first.

Then bigger ones.

Bigger.

Big, springy jumps.

And then Miss Stern saw him.

'Joshua!' she shrieked. 'Stop that at once!'

But Joshua could only shake his head.

'I'm terribly sorry,' he said, 'but I can't. I just can't. I have to keep jumping. It's how I am.'

Miss Stern was almost beside herself with rage.

'Mary!' she shouted at a girl in the class. 'Seize his left hand! Roger!' she shouted at a boy. 'Seize his right! We'll stop this foolish jumping!'

Mary did as she was told, and so did Roger.

But Joshua's jumps were so springy now that every time he jumped Mary and Roger rose into the air with him.

'Oh, this is ridiculous!' shrieked Miss Stern. 'Broderick! Take Mary's hand! Davinia! Take Roger's! We'll put an end to this!'

14   But still Joshua's jumps were too springy. And now each time he

jumped all five children rose into the air.

'Harold!' shrieked Miss Stern. 'Mavis!'

But they weren't enough either.

Miss Stern shrieked and shrieked.

And now the whole class, all holding hands in a long line with Joshua in the middle, rose into the air each time Joshua jumped.

Miss Stern ran shrieking outside.

She shrieked at this class.

That class.

The Juniors.

The Seniors.

And before long the whole school was joined in one long line with Joshua in the middle, all rising into the air each time Joshua jumped.

And Miss Stern shrieked and shrieked and didn't know what to do.

And no one cared.

Because the whole school had discovered what Joshua had always known.

Jumping makes you feel wonderful.

Absolutely wonderful.

And that's what they all did, until it was time to jump home.

Sally Farrell Odgers

A RHYME TO JUMP INTO BED WITH!

Bounda-bounda-bounda bump
Over the bushes and over the stump
Who would be walking if he could jump?
Bounda-bounda-bounda bump!

Old man wallaby sings this song
Bounda-bump as he jumps along
So does his cousin the kangaroo
'I can jump and so can you!'

Bounda-bounda-bounda bump
Over the bushes and over the stump
Who would be walking if he could jump?
Bounda-bounda-bounda bump!

Clickety-clickety-clickety hop
Once I am hoppiting I never stop
Click! through the air and I land on a rock
Clickety-clickety-clickety hop!

Green as grasshopper hops along
Clickety-click! his legs are strong
Flick! and he's gone and he's hard to see
'Bet you can't catch up with me!'

Clickety-clickety-clickety hop
Once I am hoppiting I never stop
Click! through the air and I land on a rock
Clickety-clickety-clickety hop!

Knee-deep-ee, knee-deep-ee, into the creek
This is my favourite hide-and-go-seek
I can stay hidden for over a week!
Knee-deep-ee, knee-deep-ee, into the creek.

Here comes the hoppity-floppity frog
His home is the creek and his chair is a log
He's green and he's brown and he lands with a splat!
'The mud is my bed and it's time for a nap!'

Knee-deep-ee, knee-deep-ee, into the creek
This is my favourite hide-and-go-seek
I can stay hidden for over a week!
Knee-deep-ee, knee-deep-ee, into the creek.

So sing me a song like the big kangaroo
Or croak like the frog and I'll listen to you
Tell me again what the grasshopper said
Then –
See if your jumping can land you in bed!

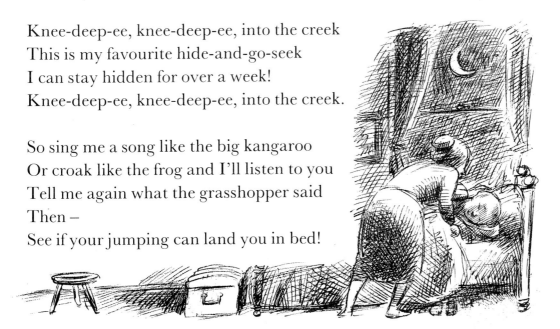

Morris Lurie

THE FROG WHO WOULD SING FOR THE KING

THERE was once a frog who loved to sing. His name was Bosphorous and he was a lovely green colour with big, bulgy eyes and he lived with all the other frogs in a large pond in a far corner of the kingdom. The pond was inky and murky and dark, though here and there dappled with sun, exactly the sort of pond that frogs love best.

'*Tra la la,*' sang Bosphorous, perched on a lily pad.

'*I sing the song of froggie swimming,*

Backstroke,

Logstroke,

Downstroke,

Frogstroke,

Oh lovely, lovely, but nothing tops,

Doing froggie belly flops!'

'Says who?' said the other frogs. 'Who says?'

'What?' said Bosphorous. 'I beg your pardon?'

'Singing is silly,' said the other frogs. 'Frogs don't sing. Frogs go *gloop.*'

'But I love to sing,' said Bosphorous. 'I have to sing. Singing is wonderful. Singing is life. And one day I shall sing for the King.'

'Sing for the King?' said the other frogs. 'Ha ha ha! Oh, don't make us laugh, Bosphorous! *Gloop gloop!*'

And into the inky dark waters of the pond they dived, leaving Bosphorous sitting on his lily pad all alone.

But Bosphorous sang on. His voice rang out rich and strong, as round as a pot, as warming as soup on a cold winter's day:

'Tra la la, tra la la,
I sing the song of deep pond bottom,
Glurpy bubbles,
Inky weeds,
Slimy worms,
Oozy reeds,
Oh what heaven when you've got 'em,
For a froggie's muddy bottom!'

'*Gloop gloop!*' went the other frogs. 'Silly Bosphorous! *Gloop gloop!*'

Now, across the hills and valleys on the other side of the kingdom, all was far from well.

In the King's castle there was a terrible scene.

'No, I can't eat this!' roared the King, hurling away his supper, which was a lovely roast goose. Splat! it went against the wall. 'I am much too angry for food!'

The King was a little man with scarlet hair and a scarlet face, and his name was King Cedric and he was always angry.

'But Your Majesty,' said the King's Adviser, 'you haven't eaten a single thing for days and days and days.'

'Yar!' roared the King, his face becoming more scarlet than ever. 'Who cares? I am too angry to eat!'

And he hurled away his salt and pepper too – bang! bang! – against the wall.

'May I advise some music, sire?' said the King's Adviser, who was tall and lean with grindy fingers and a long, crafty nose.

'Music?' roared the King. 'What music? How can you speak of music at a time like this?'

'Because music will distract you from your cares and woes,' said the King's Adviser, tapping his crafty nose. 'And you will eat your supper and feel soothed and all will be well in the kingdom.'

And he snapped his fingers and into the King's chamber strode three tall trumpeters.

Blare blare! they shrilled. *Blare blare*!

'Out!' roared the King at once. 'Out! Oh, what a dreadful noise! I feel even angrier than ever!'

'A thousand pardons, sire,' said the King's Adviser, bowing to the floor. 'My deepest apologies. Not the kind of music I intended for Your Majesty at all. But if you will allow me, sire.'

And again he snapped his fingers, and this time into the King's chamber came three small men carrying violins.

Screech screech! went the violins. *Screech screech*!

'Out!' roared the King. 'Out!'

The King was so angry this time that his face leapt from scarlet to royal purple.

'Oh, they were even more horrible than the ones before,' he cried. 'Out! Out! And you, too!' he roared at his Adviser. 'And if you can't find me the right kind of music, then you needn't bother ever coming back!'

'Yes, sire,' said the King's Adviser, scurrying backwards from the King's chamber, 'yes, sire,' bowing so low his long nose scraped the floor.

For three weeks, day and night, the King's Adviser rode about the kingdom, searching for the music to soothe his angry King. And in one village he heard the music of flutes, and in another of harps, and in a third of drums. But the drums were too noisy, and the harps were too sleepy, and the flutes were too sad.

'No,' said the King's Adviser, grinding his fingers. 'That's not the music I need for my King.'

And he had almost given up when one day he found himself by a pond. The King's Adviser was tired. He thought he would rest a while. He dismounted from his horse and sat down on the grass by the inky dark waters of the pond.

'*Gloop gloop,*' he heard all around. '*Gloop gloop.*'

'Frogs,' said the King's Adviser. 'This pond must be full of frogs.'

And then suddenly he heard something else.

'*Tra la la!*' he heard. '*Tra la la!*'

It was the song of Bosphorous, rich and strong, as round as a pot, as warming as soup.

'That's it!' cried the King's Adviser, leaping to his feet. 'That's the music I've been searching for! That's exactly it!'

In his castle, King Cedric was as angry as ever.

'Yar!' he cried, hurling away yet another dinner, six splendid roast quails this time. Splot! they went against the wall.

The King's Adviser tiptoed into the King's chamber bearing Bosphorous the frog.

'Yar!' shouted the King. 'Who is it? What do you want?'

'Sing,' whispered the King's Adviser to Bosphorous.

'Sing, Bosphorous, sing!'

'*Tra la la!*' sang Bosphorous. '*Tra la la!*'

> '*I sing the song of insect pudding,*
> *Waterbug noses,*
> *Mosquito wings,*
> *Tiny gnat knees,*
> *And suchlike things,*
> *Yum yum, yum yum,*
> *In my froggie's tum!*'

'Bring me lamb chops!' cried King Cedric. 'Bring me porridge! Bring me bananas and carrots and chocolates and stew! I am cured of my anger! I am hungry at last!'

And he commanded Bosphorous to sit beside him, on a special red velvet cushion, by the King's right hand.

'My dear Bosphorous,' said King Cedric, 'you have made me well with your joyous song, and tomorrow I shall bestow upon you the highest honour in the land. A royal banquet, filled with music and song!'

'*Tra la la!*' sang Bosphorous, bulging with happiness, as only a frog can bulge. '*Tra la la!*'

> '*I sing the song of frogs and kings,*
> *Golden goblets,*
> *Shining trumpets,*
> *Snapping banners,*
> *Toasted crumpets,*
> *Hooray for the King, exceedingly fond,*
> *And me beside him, the whole world our pond!*'

Margaret Mahy

WHEN THE KING RIDES BY

Oh, what a fuss when the King rides by
And the drum plays *rat-a-plan-plan!*

Oh, what a fuss when the King rides by –
The puss-cat runs and the pigeons fly
And the drum plays *rat-a-plan-plan!*

Oh, what a fuss when the King rides by –
The dogs all bark and the babies cry,
The puss-cat runs and the pigeons fly,
And the drum plays *rat-a-plan-plan!*

Oh, what a fuss when the King rides by –
The soldiers stamp and the ladies sigh,
The dogs all bark and the babies cry,
The puss-cat runs and the pigeons fly,
And the drum goes *rat-a-plan-plan!*

Oh, what a fuss when the King rides by –
The people throw their hats up high,
The soldiers stamp and the ladies sigh,
The dogs all bark and the babies cry,
The puss-cat runs and the pigeons fly,
And the drum goes *rat-a-plan-plan!*

Oh, what a fuss when the King rides by
Mice in their mouse-hole wonder why
The people throw their hats up high,
The soldiers stamp and the ladies sigh,
The dogs all bark and the babies cry,
The puss-cat runs and the pigeons fly,
And the drum goes *rat-a-plan-plan!*

Oh, what a fuss when the King rides by
Rockets dance in the starry sky,
Mice in their mouse-hole wonder why
The people throw their hats up high,
The soldiers stamp and the ladies sigh,
The dogs all bark and the babies cry,
The puss-cat runs and the pigeons fly,
And the drum goes *rat-a-plan-plan!*

Mavis Scott

LITTLE HO
AND THE GOLDEN KITES

LITTLE Ho woke up very early and ran to the window.

A sunny day, a windy day, for the Day of the Golden Kites!

Little Ho was very happy. Today his mother and father were taking him all the way to the Palace Gardens to see the Golden Kites.

Soon they were in the donkey cart. Down through the mountains they went. Down through the forests and rice fields and into the big city.

Little Ho had never seen the big city before. So many people. And the markets – so full of beautiful fruit and huge piles of marrows and pumpkins and bright red radishes.

Lovely smells, too, especially the smell of beancurd dumplings cooking in their pots. Little Ho's mother said he could have one after they had seen the kites. Then he could get as sticky as he liked.

They walked all through the city till they came at last to the Palace Gardens.

You should have seen those Gardens! If you'd been there you could have played hide and seek with Little Ho in the shade under the giant old trees. But you could never have counted all the flowers, or butterflies. Little Ho watched the butterflies and thought about the kites he would see and the beancurd dumpling he would eat later.

Soon it was time for all the people to gather by the steps of the Palace to see the rich nobles bring out their Golden Kites.

Little Ho heard drumbeats. The nobles were coming.

There they were!

First came Lord North Wind. His kite was like a dragon, shining golden in the sunlight.

'Aaaah!' said all the people.'That one will win the Emperor's prize.'

Next came Lord Noble Horse. His kite was like a golden eagle with its wings spread wide. It soared into the sky.

The people cheered and clapped. 'That one is the best!' they said.

Last of all came Lord Black Mountain. His kite was made like the flames from a fire, and there were rich jewels in its tail. The fire kite sparkled all over the sky.

The people cheered their loudest. 'That one wins! That one wins!' they called.

The drums beat again.

The Emperor came, dressed most wonderfully in blue and gold.

The people knelt down.

'Rise, my good people,' said the Emperor. 'Rise and enjoy these beautiful kites.'

The Emperor himself began to clap the noble lords who had made the Golden Kites, and the people clapped with him.

Now the Emperor had to choose whose kite was the best, and give his prize to the winner.

Little Ho stepped out before the Emperor. 'Please, Lord Emperor,' he said, 'I have brought my kite, too.'

The people gasped.

'How rude!' they said. 'How wrong! What a dreadful child to go near our Emperor and speak like that. His mother didn't teach him any politeness at all.'

Little Ho's mother and father sank to the ground.

'Oh,' said his mother, 'I am so ashamed. Little Ho is such a good boy. Well, nearly always . . . and now . . .' She began to cry.

The Emperor looked down at Little Ho. 'Let me see your kite,' he said gently.

Little Ho pulled his kite out from inside his jacket. It was mostly made of paper and string, but he had drawn a big smile across it, and big eyebrows and smiling eyes. He had also remembered to paint it gold, though some of the gold paint had run a little.

'A terrible, disgraceful kite,' said all the people.

Little Ho's father could not bear to look.

A soldier standing near drew his sword.

The Emperor took the kite in his hands and looked at it for a long, long time.

There was not one sound in the Gardens. Even the birds were silent.

Little Ho was afraid. He looked up. He could see two big tears running down the Emperor's cheeks, and then he heard the Emperor say quietly, 'This is my kite. I have found it again after all these years.'

'Oh, no, Lord Emperor,' said Little Ho, 'it is *my* kite. I made it all by myself and I didn't tell anyone about it. But you can have it if you like.'

The soldier stood with his sword raised above Little Ho's head. Off with the head of this rude little boy!

The Emperor raised his right hand and the soldier put down his sword.

'When I was a small boy like you,' the Emperor said, 'I made a kite just like this. I flew it in these Gardens and I was happy all day long. Then I had to grow up and learn to be an Emperor, and that was very, very hard to do. People said I must not run in the Gardens and fly kites any more. Oh, no! I must study and learn so many things that my head was spinning. I had to make laws, and learn to be good and wise. I had to sit on a throne and have wonderfully good manners all the time, and dress in stiff new clothes every day. I used to think about my kite with the smile on it, and my happy days in the Gardens. But then I began to forget a little more, and a little more, till I did not even remember where I had put my kite with the smile.'

The Emperor put his hand on Little Ho's head. 'What is your name, my clever kite-maker?' he said.

'My name is Little Ho, Lord Emperor.'

'Well then, Little Ho, shall we go to my own private garden and fly your kite together?'

'Yes, please, Lord Emperor,' said Little Ho, very happily. 'It is a good kite. It flies very well, I know. Oh, and please may I have a beancurd dumpling as well?'

'A beancurd dumpling!' said the Emperor, smiling. 'We'll both have a beancurd dumpling. You can hold them, while I have first turn to fly the kite. Do you think that is fair, Little Ho?'

'Yes, Lord Emperor. You are the Emperor and you must have first turn.'

'Mind you don't eat my dumpling by mistake,' the Emperor said.

'And now,' said the Emperor in a loud, clear voice, 'I think Lord Black Mountain wins this year.' And he gave Lord Black Mountain the prize of a bag of gold.

Of course he gave a bag of silver to Lord Noble Horse, but to Lord North Wind he gave a bag of chocolate biscuits because that's what he liked best, and he had lots of gold and silver anyway.

So that is why, every Sunday afternoon at three o'clock, Little Ho goes to the palace and flies his Kite of Smiles with the great Lord Emperor, and they both have a beancurd dumpling every time.

Colin Thiele

WHEN I WENT TO BYADUK

When I went to Byaduk, to Byaduk, to Byaduk,
My grandma said to me,
'Will you try to buy a duck, buy a duck, buy a duck,
And bring it home for tea?'

And when I went past Bessiebelle, Bessiebelle, Bessiebelle,
My grandma said to me,
'You'd better get a drake as well, drake as well, drake as well,
Or maybe two or three.'

But when I came to Drik Drik, to Drik Drik, to Drik Drik,
My grandma changed her mind:
'I think I'd like a roast chick, a roast chick, a roast chick,
And a piglet's bacon rind.'

And when I drove through Drong Drong, through Drong Drong,
    through Drong Drong,
My grandma loudly said,
'To talk of food is wrong wrong, is wrong wrong, is wrong wrong,
I want a pet instead.'

'What sort of pet from Chinkapook, Chinkapook, Chinkapook,
Is pictured in your head?'
I asked my gran in Coomandook, Coomandook, Coomandook,
And this is what she said:

'I will not take a mouse or moose, mouse or moose, mouse or moose,
Or things that purr and fuss,
What I want is not a puss, not a puss, not a puss,
And not a duck-billed platypus, platypus, platypus,
But just a hippo – hippopoto – just a hippopotamus.'

Geoffrey Dutton

THE WIND CHASE

My little sister says the wind's been chasing
Her all over the beach, and she's been racing,
Faster than spray on the waves or chimney smoke.
But now she's sleepy, and she tells me that she spoke
Very politely to the wind and said
Please would it snuggle up with her in bed.
Judging by the way this wind is blowing the sea,
I would rather have other things in bed with me.

Max Fatchen

SHELL TALK

If you hold a shell to your ear, they say,
   You'll hear the sea winds blow.
I held one to my ear. It said:
   ''Ullo, 'ullo, 'ullo.'

June Epstein

THE EARS OF MANDY

THERE was a fat grey cat who was so old that none of the children in his house could remember when he was a kitten. He was old before they were born.

He was called Mandy because someone mistook him for a girl cat, and by the time they found out he wasn't, it was too late.

He spent most of the day lying on the window seat in the living-room, or on a cushion on the back veranda. He was too old to be active, and his eyes were so bad that he could hardly see at all. But his whiskers twitched a lot.

And his ears!

That cat could hear anything and everything. You might say he lived through his ears.

His ears told him when the day started, because he heard the birds begin to sing. Then he heard the *tring tring* of the alarm,

the *creak creak* of the bed,

the *patter patter* of small feet

and the *slap slap* of Somebody's slippers.

Click went the latch of the back door, *eek eek* went its hinges, and Somebody said, 'Outside, Mandy!' And out he went.

When he was ready to come in again he gave one *miaow* at the back door.

Chink chink went the cups and saucers.

Guggle guggle went the milk as it was poured into his own special dish.

Purr purr went Mandy when he had finished his breakfast and wanted to say, 'Thank you.' He snuggled against Somebody's pyjama leg and a big warm hand stroked his fur, and he heard Somebody's voice say, 'Good puss.'

That was how Mandy's day always began.

But one morning a terrible thing happened.

He heard the birds begin to sing while it was still dark.

He waited for the alarm. There was no *tring tring*.

He waited for the bed. There was no *creak creak*.

He listened for the *patter patter* of small feet and the *slap slap* of Somebody's slippers – but nothing happened.

All was quiet for a very long time. Then he heard footsteps on the path outside the back door. *Click* went the door, *eek eek* went the hinges, and a voice said, 'Outside Mandy!' Only it wasn't Somebody's voice. Mandy knew it belonged to the boy-next-door.

Mandy would have refused to go outside. But he needed to go.

When he was ready for breakfast there was another unpleasant surprise. His special dish of milk had been placed on the back veranda instead of on the kitchen floor. 'Miaow,' said Mandy at the back door. But nobody opened it.

Mandy was insulted. He would have refused to drink the milk. But he was thirsty.

That was a terrible day. He could not hear his family at all. They had gone away. He could not get inside the house. He had to sleep all day on the cushion on the veranda.

Mandy would have refused to sleep. But he was old and tired.

At tea-time, the boy-next-door gave him some choice meat, and later he let him into the house for a while. He even said, 'Good puss,' and tried to stroke him. But his hand was so different from Some-body's that it made Mandy cross. In fact he would have scratched the

34

boy-next-door if he had not been a well-trained cat who knew his manners. Besides, he was very old.

The next day was just as bad, and the next, and the next.

On the next day after that, Mandy was lying on his cushion listening to the cars swishing along the road and the people tramping along the footpath. Suddenly something wonderful happened.

From all the different sounds in the street, Mandy's ears picked out one particular sound. His whiskers began to twitch. It was the special *vrrrm vrrrm* that he knew came only from the engine of one special car. It was Somebody's car.

Mandy listened. *Beep beep* went a horn, *slam* went a car door, *cling clang* went the gate. *Vrrrrm vrrrrm* went the car along the drive, *slam slam slam* went the car doors, *chatter chatter* went the voices. And he knew his family had come home.

Next day, Mandy woke early on his window seat in the livingroom. He did not wait to hear the birds, or the alarm, or the bed or the feet or the slippers. He forgot he was old and fat and slow. He went quickly *pit-pat pit-pat* into the bedroom, jumped onto Somebody's bed and snuggled down on the blankets. A big warm hand stroked his fur and Somebody's sleepy voice said, 'Good puss!'

Then Mandy made his own loudest, happiest special purring noise, and it was everybody else's turn to listen.

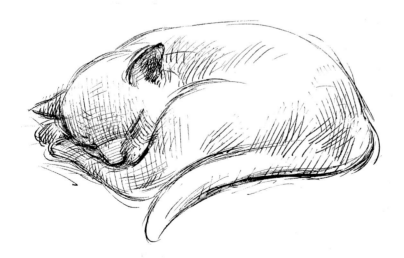

Robin Klein

NEW RED SHOES

JENNY sat in the garden at the play-centre and looked down at her new red shoes. She didn't run to play with the other children, or listen to Mrs Miller reading a picture book story.

'Come and sit with us and listen to the story, Jenny,' Mrs Miller called, but Jenny pretended not to hear. She kept her head down and looked at her new red shoes.

She knew that she would be collected at three o'clock when her mother finished work, but she still felt shy and homesick. Mrs Miller had tried to help her take off her coat and hang it on the pegs inside, but Jenny had squirmed away and gone to sit all by herself in the corner of the playground.

She looked at her new red shoes, her red tights, the hem of her checked skirt and the circle of grass where she was sitting. Sometimes another child would come up and say, 'Hello, my name's Peter' or 'Come and play skippy with us.' But Jenny just shook her head and went on staring at her new red shoes.

Mrs Miller came and took her hand and pulled her gently up. 'Come on, Jenny,' she said. 'You'll get cold sitting there like that.

36

Come and look at all the nice things we have to play with.'

Jenny was too shy to pull her hand away. Mrs Miller showed her the little pine castle. It had a tower and tunnel and was just big enough for two children to fit into, but Jenny hardly looked at it at all. She put her chin down inside the collar of her coat and kept her eyes on her new red shoes.

Mrs Miller showed her the rabbit in its hutch and the tricycles and the painting easels. 'See all the lovely things we have here?' she said. 'Don't you want to play with any of them?'

'I want to go home,' Jenny whispered. 'I don't like it here.'

But she whispered it so softly that Mrs Miller couldn't hear. And when Mrs Miller let go her hand to help someone stuck on the slippery slide, Jenny crept back to the corner of the playground and sat there, huddled up very quietly in her coat, and looked at her new red shoes.

She had chosen those shoes all by herself. It was the first time she had been allowed to choose clothes by herself, because her mother said she was a big girl now, big enough to go to play-centre. The shoes had a star pattern of tiny holes, and an ankle strap, and the buckle was shaped like a star, too. Jenny was proud of her red shoes, and wished that she wasn't shy. She wished she could go up to Mrs Miller and all the other children and say, 'Look! I chose these shoes all by myself!' But she wasn't brave enough to talk to anyone or join in any games. When any other children ran past and stopped, she kept her head down very low until they went away.

Some of the children went home at lunch time, and a different group came in the afternoon. Jenny listened to them playing wonderful, exciting games all around her, and she felt sad and lonely, sitting there all by herself and not knowing how to make friends.

'I don't care,' she said to herself.

But she did care.

Finally, someone came past and stopped. Jenny was too shy to look up to see who it was. She kept her eyes down and looked at her shoes. The other person didn't move or go away, and Jenny looked a bit further.

37

And there in the grass, in front of her red shoes, was a pair of shoes exactly the same! They had a star-shaped pattern of tiny holes, and an ankle strap, and the buckle was shaped like a star, too. Jenny looked a bit more and saw a pair of legs in red tights, just like hers. She looked a bit more and saw the hem of a checked skirt, just like hers.

'Hello,' said the somebody who owned the other red shoes and the red tights and the checked skirt. 'I'm Jessica.'

Jenny looked all the way up, because she wanted to see if Jessica had blonde hair, like hers. But Jessica had curly dark hair, and she wasn't huddled up in a coat.

'I chose my shoes all by myself,' Jenny said shyly.

'So did I,' said Jessica, 'because I'm big enough to come to play-centre now. They're good shoes for jumping on the springboard. Come on, let's jump together!'

And Jenny smiled back and got up, because that was what she had been longing to do ever since she'd arrived at the play-centre – to jump on the springboard with someone.

'I'm coming,' said Jenny. 'But first I have to take off my coat. You can't play properly in a coat.'

Margaret Mahy

FAMILY TREASURES

My daddy he died, and he left to me
A griddle, and a riddle and a fiddle-de-dee.
I cooked upon the griddle,
And I thought about the riddle,
And I played a little twiddle on my fiddle-de-dee.

When I was a grown girl I ran away to sea
With my griddle, and my riddle and my fiddle-de-dee.
People feasted at the griddle,
And they puzzled at the riddle,
Hands across and down the middle to the fiddle-de-dee.

I grew as rich as a body could be
With my griddle, and my riddle and my fiddle-de-dee.
And I sizzled at my griddle,
And I wrestled with my riddle,
Sinking deeper in the singing of my fiddle-de-dee.

Now I have a daughter, and she'll get from me
A griddle, and a riddle and a fiddle-de-dee.
She can bake upon the griddle,
She can struggle with the riddle,
And can play a different twiddle on the fiddle-de-dee!

June Epstein

ALEXANDER

ALEXANDER was a new baby. He was so new that all his aunts and uncles and cousins came to see him. Mum unwrapped him, and they counted his ten toes and ten fingers, and said how tiny and pink they were. Everyone said, 'He's beautiful!'

Everyone, that is, except his big sister, Liselotte.

Liselotte didn't think Alexander was beautiful at all. How could he be, when he had no teeth and hardly any hair? Besides that, he made wet and smelly messes in his nappy, and when he was hungry he screamed so loudly you could hear him all over the house.

Liselotte didn't wear nappies any more, even at night, and she wasn't allowed to scream. Even when she was hungry she had to say please and thank you. She had ten toes and ten fingers, like Alexander, but the aunts and uncles and cousins didn't say anything about that. They were too busy fussing over Alexander.

As soon as they went away, Liselotte said, 'I don't like Alexander. Can we put him back in your tummy?'

'No,' said Mum. 'Once a baby is born he can't go back. Alexander is your own little baby brother. You'll be able to play with him soon.'

'He's too tiny, and he's always asleep,' said Liselotte. 'I'd rather play with my doll.'

'He'll grow, and he'll wake up more,' said Mum. 'Why don't you

40

give him a cuddle? Sit on the couch and I'll put him in your lap.'

'No, I don't want to,' said Liselotte.

She put her big doll in its pram, covered it with the red check blanket Grandma had knitted, and pushed the pram outside in the garden.

That night Alexander cried. Mum changed his nappy and fed him, but he still cried. Dad walked up and down holding him, but he still cried. He was crying when Liselotte went to bed, and he was crying when she woke up. He had cried all night.

By the time the family sat down to breakfast he was screaming.

'I think you'd better sell that baby,' Dad said, as he went off to work.

'Good idea,' said Mum as she walked up and down rubbing Alexander's back.

Suddenly he gave a loud burp and in two minutes he was asleep.

Mum wrapped him up tightly in a bunny rug and put him in a basket in Liselotte's room.

'I'm worn out!' she said. 'Liselotte, you play quietly for a while and let me rest.'

She lay on the bed and in two minutes she was asleep, too.

Liselotte went to the basket and looked at Alexander. He was so tightly wrapped up that she could only see one round pink cheek and a small nose like a button.

If I could sell him, she thought, Mum wouldn't have to stay up all night.

Alexander was about the same size as Liselotte's doll, so she had no trouble lifting him out of the basket, bundle and all, and putting him in her doll's pram. She covered him with the red check blanket, and wheeled him outside and down the street.

Her friend the postman came along on his bike.

'Hello,' said Liselotte. 'Do you want to buy a baby?'

The postman looked at the bundle in the pram and thought it was Liselotte's doll.

'No thank you. I've got two of my own at home. That's quite enough for me.'

Liselotte went a little further and saw her friend Mrs Smith.

'Hello, Mrs Smith,' she said. 'Do you want to buy a baby?'

'Not today, Liselotte,' said Mrs Smith with a smile. 'You won't cross the road, will you dear?'

If I can't cross the road, Liselotte thought, how can I go to the shops to sell the baby?

Just then she saw her friend Oscar riding his tricycle up and down his drive.

It's a baby brother

'Hello, Oscar. Do you want to buy a baby?'

'Is it a girl baby or a boy baby?' asked Oscar.

'It's a baby brother.'

'Hm, I'd like one of those,' said Oscar.

'How much money have you got?' asked Liselotte.

'None,' said Oscar, 'but I'll swap him for my teddy.'

'All right,' said Liselotte. So she wheeled her doll's pram into Oscar's house, and lifted Alexander onto the couch. He was still asleep.

Oscar found his teddy under his bunk and gave it to Liselotte. She examined the teddy very carefully, the way the aunts and uncles and cousins had looked at Alexander.

'His fur's all nasty,' she said.

'That's because he fell in the bath one night,' said Oscar.

'One of his ears is coming off,' said Liselotte.

'He's nearly as old as I am,' said Oscar. 'Your mum can sew it on.'

'He hasn't got ten toes and ten fingers, like Alexander.'

'That's because he's a teddy.'

'Well, I like Alexander better than your teddy,' said Liselotte.

'You can't change back,' said Oscar.

'Yes I can.'

'You can't have him.'

'I can *so*!' said Liselotte, throwing the teddy on the floor. She went to get Alexander, but Oscar stood in front of the couch.

'Move away! I want my baby brother! He's mine!' Liselotte shouted.

She shouted so loudly that Oscar's mum came running in to see what was wrong.

'Liselotte! Does your mother know you're here?' She saw the bundle on the couch and lifted the bunny rug from Alexander's face. She gave a little scream. 'Liselotte! Did you bring that baby here?'

'My mum and dad want to sell him,' said Liselotte.

'What nonsense! Come home with me at once. Your mother must be out of her mind with worry.' And she scooped up Alexander and scurried along the street with Liselotte running behind, pushing her doll's pram, and Oscar chasing them on his tricycle. Teddy was left behind on the floor.

Liselotte's mum had just woken up, found the empty basket, and dashed out into the street. There she saw Oscar's Mum clutching the baby, Liselotte running along behind with the pram, and Oscar pedalling hard on his tricycle.

'You naughty girl, Liselotte!' she said, grabbing Alexander. 'Why on earth did you take him?'

Alexander was still asleep.

'You said you wanted to sell him,' said Liselotte.

'Of course we wouldn't sell him!' said her mother. 'It was a joke!'

When they had all calmed down a little, she said thank you to

43

Oscar's mum for bringing the baby home, and she and Liselotte went inside the house where Mum tucked Alexander back in his basket.

'Liselotte,' she said, 'stop crying and listen to me. You must never *never* pick up Alexander without asking. He is so soft and tiny you could hurt him without meaning to.'

Liselotte said in a very small voice, 'Will you sell me, now you've got Alexander?'

'Never, never, *never*!' said Mum. 'You're our special little girl; the best in the whole world.' And she gave Liselotte a big hug.

'I didn't hurt him, did I?' asked Liselotte.

'No, he's all right, he didn't even know he was kidnapped. Come and see,' said Mum, and she unwrapped the bunny rug.

Alexander was just waking up. His blue stretch suit covered his toes, but he waved his fists, and Liselotte looked at his ten tiny pink fingers. He gave a huge yawn, and she saw his mouth without any teeth. Then he opened his eyes, and when he saw Liselotte bending over him his mouth stretched wide and this time he wasn't yawning.

'He's *smiling*!' said Liselotte's mum. 'His very first smile, and it's for you, Liselotte!'

Liselotte put her finger into Alexander's hand and his tiny fingers curled round and held it tight.

She said, 'He's beautiful!'

Doug MacLeod

STOMPING HORACE

Horace was a stomper
In the second grade.
Horace stomped on sandcastles,
Ones he hadn't made.

Children at the seaside
Prayed they wouldn't meet
Horace with his huge, horrendous,
Hefty stomping feet.

Crushing sandy fortresses,
Horace thought it clever.
Empires rose and empires fell
But *he* stomped on forever.

Through the conquered kingdoms
Horace loved to romp
Till the day that Horace
Stomped his final stomp.

There's the place it happened,
Near it is a sign
Horace failed to notice:
UNEXPLODED MINE.

C. J. Dennis

THE ANT EXPLORER

Once a little sugar ant made up his mind to roam –
To fare away far away, far away from home.
He had eaten all his breakfast, and he had his Ma's consent
To see what he should chance to see and here's the way he went –
Up and down a fern frond, round and round a stone,
Down a gloomy gully where he loathed to be alone,
Up a mighty mountain range, seven inches high,
Through the fearful forest grass that nearly hid the sky,
Out along a bracken bridge, bending in the moss,
Till he reached a dreadful desert that was feet and feet across.
'Twas a dry, deserted desert, and a trackless land to tread;
He wished that he was home again and tucked-up tight in bed.
His little legs were wobbly, his strength was nearly spent
And so he turned around again and here's the way he went –
Back away from desert lands feet and feet across,
Back along the bracken bridge bending in the moss,
Through the fearful forest grass, shutting out the sky,
Up a mighty mountain range seven inches high,
Down a gloomy gully, where he loathed to be alone,
Up and down a fern frond and round and round a stone,
A dreary ant, a weary ant, resolved no more to roam,
He staggered up the garden path and popped back home.

Anon.

TEN LITTLE RABBITS

Ten little Rabbits playing round a mine
One slipped down a shaft, then there were nine.
Nine little Rabbits hopping through a gate,
One caught in a snare, then there were eight.
Eight little Rabbits gazing up to Heaven,
Down swooped an eagle-hawk, then there were seven.
Seven little Rabbits up to their tricks,
When a red fox grabbed one, then there were six.
Six little Rabbits hunted in a drive,
One got a dose of shot, then there were five.
Five little Rabbits drinking round a bore,
One got squirted up, then there were four.
Four little Rabbits scratching round a tree,
One ate a quince-jam bait, then there were three.
Three little Rabbits saw a jackeroo,
One got asphyxiated, then there were two.
Two little Rabbits flirting in the sun,
A goanna gave a swallow, then there was one.
One little Rabbit feeling lonely when
She had a family, and again there were ten.

Sally Farrell Odgers

HIGHRISE

Do you know what I would build
If all the blocks were mine?
I'd pile them up
And pile them up
As high as I could climb.
I'd put the red ones first, of course,
That's where they'd have to be,
I'd pile them up
And pile them up
Higher up than me!
The blocks would cover half the lawn
(I'd do my work outside);
I'd pile them up
And pile them up
And spread them really wide.
And when I'd built with all the red,
I'd use the yellow ones;
I'd pile them up
And pile them up
I reckon there'd be tonnes!
Then I'd have the blue and green
Sent to me in planes.
I'd pile them up
And pile them up
And pile them up again.
And when I'd get to purple blocks
I'd need a crane to reach,
I'd pile them up

And pile them up
Above the blocks beneath.
When the orange blocks were gone
I'd start to use the grey;
I'd pile them up
And pile them up
A very clever way.
And all the blocks in all the world
Would soon be sent to me;
I'd pile them up
And pile them up
As high as you could see!
And when my blocks had disappeared
Into the whitest clouds,
I'd pile them up
And pile them up
And then would you be proud?
And I would save a special one
The very best of blocks;
I'd clamber up
And clamber up
And put it at the top.
Then –
    All the people in the world
    Would come to see our town;
    I'd show my blocks to *everyone* –
    And then I'd knock them down!
CRASH!

FRIGHTENING THE MONSTER
IN WIZARD'S HOLE

ONE day a truckload of bricks went over a bump and two bricks fell off into the middle of the road. They lay there like two new-laid oblong eggs dropped by some unusual bird. A boy called Tom-Tom, coming down the road, stopped to look at them. He picked one up. It was a beautiful glowing orange coloured brick and it seemed as if it should be used for something special, but what can you do that's special with only one brick or even two?

'Hey Tom-Tom!' called his friend Sam Bucket, coming up behind him. 'What are you doing with that brick?'

'Just holding it,' Tom-Tom said, 'holding it and thinking . . .'

'Thinking what?'

'. . . thinking that I'd take it and throw it really hard at . . .'

'At whom, Tom-Tom?'

'At the monster in Wizard's Hole.'

Sam's eyes and mouth opened like early morning windows. 'You'd be too scared.'

50

'No I wouldn't! That's what I'm going to do now.'

Tom-Tom set off down the road with his bright orange brick. Sam Bucket did not see why Tom-Tom should have all the glory and adventure. He grabbed the brick that was left in the middle of the road.

'Hang on Tom-Tom! I'm coming too.'

'Okay!' said Tom-Tom grandly. 'But don't forget it's my idea, so I'm going to throw first.'

'Where're you two off to?' asked a farmer, leaning over his gate.

'We're going to throw these bricks at the monster in Wizard's Hole,' explained Tom-Tom.

'He's going to throw first and I'm going to throw next,' cried Sam boastfully.

'You'd never dare!' cried the farmer.

'We're on our way now,' they said together, strutting like bantam roosters along the sunny dusty road.

'But how are you going to get the monster out of Wizard's Hole?' asked the farmer. 'He hasn't looked out for years.'

'I shall shout at him,' declared Tom-Tom grandly. 'I shall say, "Come on, Monster, out you come!" and he'll have to come, my voice will be so commanding.'

'I shall shout too,' said Sam Bucket quickly. '"Come out, Monster," I shall say. "Come out and have bricks thrown at you." My voice will be like a lion's roar. He'll have to come.'

'Hang on a moment,' said the farmer. 'I've got a brick down here for holding my gate open. I'm coming too.'

Off went Tom-Tom, Sam Bucket and the farmer, all holding bricks, all marching with a sense of purpose. They passed Mrs Puddenytame's Pumpkin farm where Mrs Puddenytame herself was out subduing the wild twining pumpkins.

'You lot look pleased with yourselves,' she remarked as they went by.

'We are,' said Tom-Tom, 'because we're on our way to do great things. You see these bricks? We're on our way to throw them at the monster in Wizard's Hole.'

'You'd never dare!' breathed Mrs Puddenytame. 'Why, they say that the monster is all lumpy and bumpy, horrible, hairy and hideous – and besides, he hasn't bothered anyone for a hundred years.'

'"Come out," we'll say, "out you come, Monster, and have bricks thrown at you."'

'He'll have to come,' cried the farmer. 'And when he feels our bricks he'll run like a rabbit. We'll be heroes to the whole country.'

'Well, hang on then!' Mrs Puddenytame shouted. 'I've got a few spare bricks myself – and seven sons too.' And she hunted the sons out of the pumpkins shouting, 'Come on you louts! You can be heroes too.'

'But Mother,' said the eldest, cleverest son, 'nobody else wants Wizard's Hole. Why shouldn't the monster stay there?'

'He's a monster, isn't he?' yelled Mrs Puddenytame. 'Who ever heard of rights for monsters. You get a brick and come along with the rest of us.'

Off they went, eleven people all carrying bricks down the sunny dusty road to town.

Once they got to town people came out of their houses to watch them. People followed them down the road. There was quite a procession by the time they reached the town square with the fountain in the middle of it. There Tom-Tom made a speech.

'Friends,' he cried, 'the time has come to act. We are going to throw bricks at the monster in Wizard's Hole.'

'We're going to roar like lions,' added Sam Bucket.

'And stamp like bulls!' agreed the farmer stamping.

'We're going to laugh like hyenas, and shriek like mad parrots,' Mrs Puddenytame shouted, 'and frighten the monster into the next country. We've had the monster for too long. Let someone else have him.'

'Hooray!' shouted all the people.

'The monster will run . . .' promised Tom-Tom.

'He'll flee!' agreed Sam Bucket.

'He'll fly!' gloated the farmer.

'He'll bound and pound and turn head over head over heels!' declared Mrs Puddenytame, weighing her brick in her hand.

'I think I'll get a brick too,' said the mayor thoughtfully, looking at a truckload of bricks parked by a building construction site. 'Nothing should be done without a mayor.'

'Don't forget the school children!' cried an anxious teacher. 'Remember they're the citizens of tomorrow.'

'But what are we doing it for?' asked a small child, surprised.

'For the good of the community. Go and find a brick!' commanded the teacher.

Soon everyone had taken a brick from the back of the truck and was marching sternly towards Wizard's Hole.

The monster was just sitting down to a breakfast of fried eggs and crisp bacon when he heard the sound of many feet marching towards his front door.

'Visitors – at last!' thought the monster. He rushed to his bed cave, put on a collar and tie, washed behind his ears and brushed his many teeth. Then he ran to his front door and put his head out of Wizard's Hole.

54

'Good morning!' he said and smiled.

Everyone stopped. Tom-Tom stopped, Sam Bucket stopped. The farmer, Mrs Puddenytame and her seven sons, the mayor and the school teacher – everyone stopped.

'Come on in . . . I'm just making fresh coffee.' The monster smiled again showing his newly brushed teeth. He had a lot of teeth, this monster, many of them green and all of them sharp. Everyone stared.

'Do come in. I'm so pleased to see you,' wheedled the monster. But the monster was wheedling in monster language which is a mixture of growling, whining, roaring and shrieking. Every single person dropped his brick. Every single solitary person ran without looking back once.

'Goodness me!' said the monster looking at the bricks. 'Are all these presents for me? Too kind! Too kind! Thank you . . .' he called after them. But he said the 'thank you' in monster language which is a mixture of rumbling, snarling and screaming. Everyone ran even faster than ever before.

The monster went in and put on his bricklayer's apron, got his bricklayer's trowel and made himself a handsome brick monster house. Then he moved out of Wizard's Hole, which had always been so damp that the wallpaper peeled off, and he lived happily ever after.

And when Tom-Tom heard what had happened he said, 'Well, we got him out of Wizard's Hole, any way,' and felt very successful.

E.R.

GOOSEY, GOOSEY GANDER

Goosey, Goosey Gander,
Whither do you wander?
Your place is in the poultry-yard,
And not on the veranda.

J.H.

SIX FAT GEESE

Six fat geese were grazing by the shore,
They gobbled up grass till they could eat no more.
One flew east and one flew west,
And one flew onto a bulldog's nest.
One flew north and one flew south,
One flew into a dingo's mouth.
The one that flew east fell into the sea,
The one that flew west stuck in a mulga tree.
The one that flew south had a long way to go,
And then got smothered in drifting snow.
The one that flew north was the fattest of the lot,
So I twisted her neck and put her in the pot.

Colin Thiele

WADDLE DUCK

Ducks in the farmyard, ducks in the dawnlight,
Waking up brightly as the day comes back,
Waddle duck, waddle duck,
Quack, quack, quack.

Man in the morning, walking out briskly,
Heading for the yard with a bin full of mash,
Jostle duck, jostle duck,
Dash, dash, dash.

Grain on the muddy ground all in a jumble,
Frenzied feet trampling fast and thick,
Gobble duck, gobble duck,
Quick, quick, quick.

Gates swinging open, ducks free to wander,
Rushing to the river and tumbling in,
Paddle duck, paddle duck,
Swim, swim, swim.

Ducks on the water, heads tucked under,
Thinking of earthworms in the weeds and ooze,
Dreamy duck, dreamy duck,
Snooze, snooze, snooze.

Mother duck nesting, gone into hiding,
Sitting on her eggs in a thick reed patch,
Broody duck, broody duck,
Hatch, hatch, hatch.

Ducklings like yellow balls down by the river,
Ducklings watched greedily by eagle and cat,
Hurry duck, hurry duck,
Skitter, skitter, scat.

Fox in the reedbeds edging the water,
Slinking through the rushes like a whispering breeze,
Danger duck, danger duck,
Freeze, freeze, freeze.

Fox in the shadows, bright eyes shining,
Fox tensed ready with teeth like knives,
Fly ducks, *fly* ducks,
Fly for your lives.

Farmer hears the rumpus, comes out running,
Farmer sees the fox and grabs his gun,
Hurry fox, hurry fox,
Run, run, run.

Ducks safely rescued, ducks out of danger,
Sheltered by the gate and the mesh of the yard,
Learn ducks, learn ducks,
Hard, hard, hard.

Darkness and silence, peace in the night-time,
Wheeling stars wink where the Milky Way goes,
Settle ducks, settle ducks,
Doze, doze, doze.

Ducks in the farmyard hear the dawn calling,
Everything stirring as the day comes back –
So waddle duck, dawdle duck,
Quack, quack, quack;
So gobble duck, toddle duck,
Jostle and juggle duck,
Paddle duck, puddle duck,
Waddle-at-the-double duck,
Quack, quack, quack.

Bill Scott

THREE FLEAS

Here are three fleas with powerful knees
who can leap as high as the tallest trees – *boing – boing – boing!*

This is the mouse with the thoughtful frown
who was home for the fleas when they settled down;
three little fleas with powerful knees
who could leap as high as the tallest trees – *boing – boing – boing!*

This is the dingo, hungry and brown
who gobbled the mouse with the thoughtful frown
who was home for the fleas with powerful knees
who could leap as high as the tallest trees –
(guess where the fleas have gone!)

This is the man with the wrinkled forehead
who trapped the dingo, hungry and brown
who gobbled the mouse who was home to the fleas –
three little fleas with powerful knees –
(guess where the fleas are now!)

This is the bunyip, green and horrid
who gulped the man with the wrinkled forehead
who trapped the dingo hungry and brown
who gobbled the mouse with the thoughtful frown
who was home for the fleas when the sun went down –
three little fleas with powerful knees
who could leap as high as the tallest trees,
with ease.

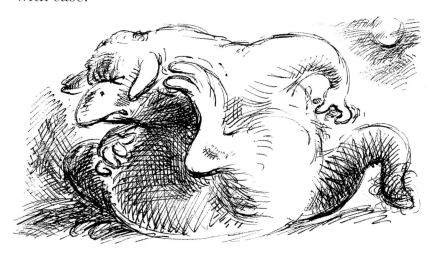

A bunyip who is a nasty sight,
whose hair and whiskers are turning white
who wriggles and scratches and kicks and bites
because he can't get any sleep at nights –
there are fleas that worry and fleas that tease,
three little fleas with muscular knees
who can leap as high as the tallest trees
and change their home with the greatest of ease –

You know where those fleas are now!

A story from Java
retold by Barbara Ker Wilson

OLD MAN CROCODILE

OLD man Crocodile lay in the shallow, muddy river, under the noonday sun. A Carrion Crow alighted on a branch of a tree that grew beside the river. He looked at old man Crocodile, and his mouth watered. 'What a wonderful feast I would enjoy with my relatives if only I could kill the Crocodile!' he thought.

'Ho there, old man Crocodile!' he called. 'What a stick-in-the-mud you are! Why do you stay in this shallow river all the time? Don't you know there is a much deeper river only a short distance from here?'

Old man Crocodile opened one eyelid. 'I have never heard of such a river,' he grunted sleepily.

'I am only telling you the truth,' said the cunning Crow. 'I want to help you.'

Old man Crocodile opened his other eyelid. 'Hm, I should like to see this other river. Will you show me the way, Master Crow?'

'Oh yes, I'll show you the way,' replied the Crow. 'It isn't far. I'm sure a big, strong creature like yourself will be able to walk there easily.'

So old man Crocodile heaved himself on to the river bank. The Crow spread his glossy back feathers and flew ahead of him. Slowly the Crocodile followed the Crow.

After they had been travelling a while, he began to groan. 'We have come a long way, Master Crow. Is it much farther to your river?'

'We are nearly there,' replied the Crow. 'Surely a big strong creature like yourself cannot be feeling tired already?'

The Crocodile felt ashamed of his tiredness. He stumbled on, still following the Crow. But at last he could go no further; he collapsed and lay helpless on the ground.

'I cannot go on, Master Crow; I am quite exhausted!' he moaned.

The Crow flew above old man Crocodile's head, laughing at him and mocking. 'What a stupid Crocodile you are! You should have stayed at home. There is no other river! You will soon die here from starvation and thirst. Then I will come and eat you up!' And he flew away to tell all his relations to prepare themselves for a wonderful feast of crocodile meat.

Presently, however, a kind-hearted villager came upon the scene, driving a bullock-cart. The crocodile begged him to save his life and take him back to his river.

'Please help me!' he cried.

The villager felt sorry for old man Crocodile. But he knew that crocodiles are not to be trusted. So, before he put him in the cart, he bound his jaws together with a strong rope. Then he drove his cart back to the shallow muddy river.

'Kind master,' said the Crocodile, 'I am so weak after my unfortunate experience that I have not strength enough to crawl into the water. Please drive your cart into the river and drop me there.'

The villager thought there could be no harm in this, so he whipped up the bullocks and drove his cart into the river, where he untied the Crocodile's jaws and pushed him into the water. At once that wicked old man Crocodile opened his jaws wide and caught hold of one of the bullock's legs with his sharp teeth.

'Let go, you ungrateful creature!' cried the villager.

But old man Crocodile took no notice, for he was very hungry.

At that moment, a Rabbit came down to the river to drink. He saw what was happening, and shouted, 'Hit the Crocodile with your driving stick! Hit him hard!'

The villager did as he was told. He hit the Crocodile so hard that he

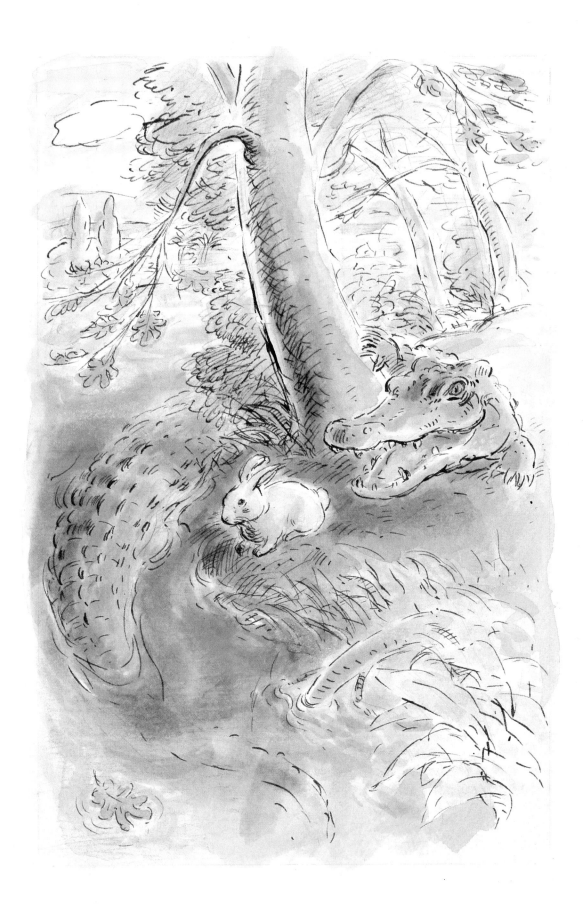

let go of the bullock. Then he drove his cart back to the bank and thanked the Rabbit for his good advice.

Old man Crocodile was very angry. 'But for that interfering Rabbit,' he said to himself, 'I should have enjoyed a good meal of bullock.' He decided to catch the Rabbit, and watched and waited for him to come again to the river to drink.

The Rabbit came to the river the very next day. Old man Crocodile lurked at the river's edge. But the water was so shallow that only his head and tail were submerged; his back remained exposed. He stayed quite still, hoping the Rabbit would mistake him for a log. But the Rabbit was wise; he looked at the strange log in the water and said aloud, 'If that were really a log, it would float downstream.'

At once the Crocodile swam a little way downstream, just to convince the Rabbit that he was indeed a log. The Rabbit seized his opportunity and drank quickly while the Crocodile was out of the way.

'You can't catch me, old man Crocodile!' he shouted as he scampered back home.

The Crocodile was furious. 'We'll see about that!' he said.

The next day he lurked once more by the river's edge and waited for the Rabbit. Once again the Rabbit saw the Crocodile's back above the water, and said aloud, 'If that were really a log, it would float downstream.'

This time the Crocodile stayed perfectly still.

'It must be a log after all!' the Rabbit thought to himself; and he put down his little head to drink.

Snap! Old man Crocodile caught hold of the Rabbit in his cruel jaws. He did not eat him at once, however. He wanted all the other animals to know how clever he had been to outwit the wise Rabbit. He swam up and down the river, laughing and shouting with glee. 'Hee, hee, hee! Clever me! Hee, hee, hee! Clever me!'

Even though he was inside the Crocodile's mouth, the Rabbit kept his wits about him. 'You stupid old Crocodile,' he cried scornfully. 'We all know you can shout "Hee, hee, hee." Anyone can do that. But can you shout "Ha, ha, ha"?'

'Of course I can!' the Crocodile replied indignantly. 'Ha, ha, ha!'

But in order to shout 'Ha, ha, ha' he had to open his jaw as wide as he could. In a flash the Rabbit jumped out of his mouth and was soon safely on dry land once more.

How angry old man Crocodile was! He thrashed his tail and wept big crocodile tears of rage. But he never had another chance to catch the clever little Rabbit.

D. H. Souter

THE CLEVER RABBIT

There was a little Rabbit
who was lying in his burrow . . .
when the Dingo rang him up to say
he'd call on him tomorrow . . .

But the Rabbit thought it better
that the Dingo did not meet him;
so he found another burrow
and the Dingo didn't eat him.

Mary Roberts

JOHN'S TASK

A POOR farmer once fell into debt to a wealthy landowner. He trembled lest he be thrown into prison and not be able to work his smallholding. He felt even worse when the landowner came to visit him.

'You deserve to go to prison,' the landowner said. 'But I am not an unjust man. See here, I will give you and your family a chance. Seven of my fields are badly overgrown with thistles. They must be cut.'

'Certainly, sir. At once, sir. I'll clear your fields this very day.'

'Not you, you fool. You are already becoming slow and stiff. Lend me your son. If he can clear my fields in seven days, I will forgive you your debt. If not, the boy can remain as my servant for life.'

John, the boy, was dearly loved by his parents and already a great help to his father. He insisted on going with the landowner.

'Don't you see, Father, what a good chance this is to free our farm from debt? I am young and strong. Only one field a day – that will be easy. Just lend me your scythe and your stone and I'll be gone. Look out for me in a week's time. And have something special in the pot for our supper, Mother.'

It was high summer, and even before sunrise next day John was up, had eaten the meagre breakfast of bread and milk left on the landlord's kitchen table, filled his leather bottle with water and put a hunk of bread inside his shirt for lunch. He put the scythe over his shoulder and strode out over the dewy grass. The field was choked and purple

70

with thistles. They nodded their fluffy heads and raised their cruel thorny fingers as if to mock him, but John bent to his task with a will. At every stroke the proud purple heads bowed and fell.

Larks rose, singing in the clear air; the sun strode over the sky. The day grew hotter and hotter. Soon John was bathed in sweat. Dust and flying downy seeds choked his nose and throat. His head felt about to burst.

'Slow down, you fool,' he told himself, 'slow and steady wins the race.'

But even though he took more time and worked rhythmically, as the day wore on he grew sick with the blistering heat, and his legs trembled beneath him.

By evening the field was clear – all but a small patch near the gate.

John was glad to bolt down a poor meal of thin stew and bread and then throw himself on his hard bed to sleep.

Next day he was stiff and his hands blistered, but he worked on grimly. A hawk hovered overhead, waiting to swoop on the fieldmice John disturbed from their thistle homes. Crows mocked him from the hedges. By nightfall, the second field was only three-quarters cleared and the landowner sneered as he came to inspect the work.

'You'll need to smarten yourself up, lad, at this rate. And mind you cut all the thistles. Look over there, you've missed a patch. Big thistles from little thistles grow, you know.'

Poor John. Struggle as he might, strive all he could, each day he found the task becoming too great. Although now he had wisely learnt to lie in the shade at noon and his body was accustomed to the rhythm of the scythe, he knew the last three fields were even larger than the first four. 'To work for this man for ever, how could I bear it?' he thought.

On the fifth day the hawk, lazily circling overhead, suddenly dropped and in one swift movement caught up a baby rabbit in its great claws. John shouted and whirled the scythe over his head. Startled, the hawk dropped its prey. The baby rabbit lay stunned and John put his hand over it to protect it. He saw the cruel, tawny eyes of the hawk as it circled low once more and then flew slowly away.

72

'You poor little fellow,' said John, uncovering the rabbit, whose eyes were bulging with terror. Gently, he put it down in the grass. With a sudden bound the rabbit was gone.

On the last night of the week John hardly slept. Every time he closed his eyes he saw row after row of thistles pushing closer and closer, thistles that refused the bite of steel and remained upright and defiant. His cruel master was up early and gloated as he watched the boy trudge stubbornly out to work. One day left and two whole fields to cut.

'I'll just have to work like a demon, even if it kills me,' John told himself as he pushed open the rough gate in the stone wall.

He stopped, gasped and rubbed his eyes. The field was bare of thistles. Each one lay wilting among the thick grass. John ran to the last field. It, too, was clear, but under the gate were squeezing dozens and dozens of rabbits – big old bucks, fat does, soft-eyed babies. Their white scuts bobbed in the grass. They were gone.

John stayed all day in the fields, trimming every furrow so that not one purple top could be seen. At nightfall he called the landowner, who was angry and puzzled, yet kept his bargain.

And in later years, when John farmed his own land, no rabbits were ever trapped and no thistles ever grew.

A Celtic story
retold by Barbara Ker Wilson

THE FOOLISH FARMER

ONCE there was a foolish farmer. His name was Mr Farmer Plod-and-plough, and he lived with Mrs Farmer Plod-and-plough in a little farmhouse with a red roof and a green front door. One day, Mrs Farmer Plod-and-plough said to her husband, 'You must go to market to sell the red cow. Mind you get a good price for her. She is worth a lot of money.'

Mr Farmer Plod-and-plough went into the field behind the farmhouse, where the red cow was grazing. 'Hup, hup, my lass,' he said, 'today we're going to market.'

And he took a rope and led the red cow along the dusty white road to the market town.

When he reached the market, he soon met a man who wanted to buy the red cow. 'That's a fine beast you have there,' the man said. 'I will give you a bag of golden coins if you will sell her to me.'

'Done!' said Mr Farmer Plod-and-plough; and so the red cow was sold.

Mr Farmer Plod-and-plough felt very pleased with himself as he walked away with the bag of golden coins in his hand. He did not know that he could have got a much better price for the red cow if he had not sold her to the first person he had met.

A crowd of people was gathered in the market square, listening to a man who was making music on the bagpipes. Every time he came to

the end of a tune, the people would clap and throw lots of silver into the man's bonnet.

'That is a good way to make money!' thought Mr Farmer Plod-and-plough. 'If only I had some bagpipes, I would soon have a hatful of silver, too!' Then he had an idea. He went up to the man and said, 'Will you give me your bagpipes in exchange for this bag of golden coins?'

'Certainly!' said the man. And he gave his bagpipes to Mr Farmer Plod-and-plough, and went off with the bag of coins. Now Mr Farmer Plod-and-plough began to blow the bagpipes. But he found he could not play any tunes at all. He could only make horrible squeaky noises, and no one threw any silver into his hat. 'Go away!' they shouted. 'We don't want to hear such a dreadful din!'

Mr Farmer Plod-and-plough felt very sad, and his fingers felt cold from holding the bagpipes. He saw a man in the crowd who was wearing a pair of thick woolly gloves. 'Will you give me your gloves in exchange for my bagpipes?' he asked the man.

'Certainly!' the man replied, delighted with the bargain.

Mr Farmer Plod-and-plough started to walk home again along the dusty white road. It had been a long day, and he felt tired. Then he saw a man coming towards him, leaning on a stout stick.

'Will you give me your stick in exchange for my woolly gloves?' he asked the man.

'Certainly!' the man replied, thinking how foolish Mr Farmer Plod-and-plough must be to part with his warm gloves for a stick that he could easily have cut from the hedge for himself.

'That's better!' thought Mr Farmer Plod-and-plough as he went on his way, leaning on the stout stick.

Soon he came home to the little farmhouse with the red roof and the green front door. Mrs Farmer Plod-and-plough was waiting for him. No sooner had he set foot inside the door than she said, 'Well! Did you sell the red cow?'

'Yes, I did,' answered Mr Farmer Plod-and-plough. 'A man gave me a bag of golden coins for her.'

'Show me them.'

'I can't do that, because I exchanged the golden coins for some bagpipes.'

'Bagpipes!' cried Mrs Farmer Plod-and-plough. 'That was a foolish thing to do. Show me the bagpipes.'

'I can't do that, because I exchanged the bagpipes for a pair of woolly gloves.'

'Woolly gloves!' exclaimed Mrs Farmer Plod-and-plough. 'You are the stupidest man alive! Show me the gloves.'

'I can't do that, because I exchanged the gloves for this stick.' And Mr Farmer Plod-and-plough showed his wife the stout stick he had leant on as he walked home.

'A stick!' shrieked Mrs Farmer Plod-and-plough. 'You walk out of here this morning with our red cow, and you return this evening with a stick you could have cut from any hedge! Oh, oh, oh!' And with that she seized the stick from her husband, and began to beat him with it. Bang! Crash! Thwack! 'Take that and that and that!' she cried.

Mr Farmer Plod-and-plough never forgot the day he went to market to sell the red cow!

Irene Gough

ROCK WALLABY

'Wallaby, wallaby
What do you eat,
Dancing the hills
On your nimble feet?'

'A berry, a leaf
And a saltbush spray
Down by the spring
At dawn of day.'

Virginia Ferguson

THE HUNGRY BUNYIP

LONG ago, in the Australian bush, there lived a farmer and his wife and a bunyip. The bunyip was their pet, and they kept him in a shed at the back of the house. The man liked food and so did his wife – but you should have seen the bunyip eat! This is what he had for breakfast:

four meat pies with sauce,

three saucepans of porridge,

two buckets of milk,

and one sack of ripe apples.

By the end of the day there wasn't a scrap of food left in the house. The man and his wife grew thinner and thinner, while the bunyip ate them out of house and home.

'I think he'll have to go,' said the farmer.

The next morning, the bunyip met the farmer and his wife filling a bucket of water near the windmill.

'Good morning, Farmer. Good morning, Wife.'

'Good morning, Bunyip. Have you eaten yet?'

'Yes, but I'm still hungry,' said the bunyip. 'I've only had:

four meat pies with sauce,

three saucepans of porridge,

two buckets of milk,

and one sack of ripe apples . . .

so if you don't mind, I think I'll eat you, too.'

He opened his mouth and gobbled up the farmer and his wife. Then he ran to the cowshed where the cow was mooing, waiting to be milked.

'Good morning, Cow,' said the bunyip.

'Good morning, Bunyip. Have you eaten yet?'

'Yes, but I'm still hungry,' said the bunyip. 'I've only had:

four meat pies with sauce,

three saucepans of porridge,

two buckets of milk,

one sack of ripe apples,

and the farmer and his wife . . .

so if you don't mind, I think I'll eat you, too.'

He opened his mouth and gobbled up the cow.

In a cloud of dust a drover rode up on his horse, followed by a whole herd of cattle.

'Good morning, Drover.'

'Good morning, Bunyip. Have you eaten yet?'

'Yes, but I'm still hungry,' said the bunyip. 'I've only had:

four meat pies with sauce,

three saucepans of porridge,

two buckets of milk,

one sack of ripe apples,

the farmer and his wife,

and the cow . . .

so if you don't mind, I think I'll eat you, too.'

He opened his mouth and gobbled up the drover, his horse and the whole herd of cattle.

A flock of sheep was standing by a tree full of kookaburras.

'Good morning, sheep. Good morning, kookaburras.'

'Good morning, Bunyip. Have you eaten yet?'

'Yes, but I'm still hungry,' said the bunyip. 'I've only had:

>   four meat pies with sauce,
>
>   three saucepans of porridge,
>
>   two buckets of milk,
>
>   one sack of ripe apples,
>
>   the farmer and his wife,
>
>   the cow,
>
>   and the drover, his horse and his whole herd of cattle . . .

so if you don't mind, I think I'll eat you, too.'

He opened up his mouth and gobbled up the sheep and the tree full of kookaburras.

The bunyip came to a school.

'Good morning, children,' said the bunyip.

'Good morning, Bunyip,' sang the children. 'Have you eaten yet?'

'Yes, but I'm still hungry,' said the bunyip. 'I've only had:

>   four meat pies with sauce,
>
>   three saucepans of porridge,
>
>   two buckets of milk,
>
>   one sack of ripe apples,
>
>   the farmer and his wife,
>
>   the cow,
>
>   the drover, his horse and his whole herd of cattle,
>
>   and a flock of sheep and a tree full of kookaburras . . .

so if you don't mind, I think I'll eat you, too.'

'Eat the teacher first,' cried the children.

So the bunyip opened his mouth and gobbled up the teacher.

'Hurrah!' shouted the children. But then he gobbled them up as well.

A shearer's cook saw this happen. The bunyip didn't like the look of the angry cook.

The cook yelled, 'What made you do such an awful thing? Why did you eat the teacher and a whole school of children?'

'I was hungry,' cried the bunyip.

'Hungry?' roared the cook. 'What have you eaten today?'

'Not very much,' cried the bunyip, trembling with fright. 'I've only had:

four meat pies with sauce,

three saucepans of porridge,

two buckets of milk,

one sack of ripe apples,

the farmer and his wife,

the cow,

the drover, his horse and his whole herd of cattle,

a flock of sheep and a tree full of kookaburras,

and a teacher and a whole school of children . . .'

'Well, don't think you can eat me, too,' said the shearer's cook. 'Why don't you try a billy of my special shearer's stew?'

He heated the stew but the bunyip didn't see him put in half a bucket of pepper.

'Open wide,' said the shearer's cook, and he poured it down the bunyip's throat.

People in a town far away thought a cyclone was coming. All the thunderstorms in the world couldn't sound as loud as the sneezes which came from the bunyip's burning nose.

Ah choo! – and out jumped the school teacher and the whole school of children.

'Finish your work before you go out to play,' she said.

Ah choo! – out flew the tree full of kookaburras.

Ah choo! – out leapt the flock of sheep.

Ah choo! – out rode the drover on his horse, droving his herd of cattle.

Ah choo! – out jumped the cow, still mooing to be milked.

Ah choo! Ah choo! – and out shot the farmer and his wife.

The farmer's wife milked the cow, the farmer went off to work on his farm, and everyone lived happily ever after.

But the bunyip was never seen again.

J. S. Manifold

M. M.'s SONGS

Coots eat waterbeetles,
Rats eat cheese,
Goats eat anything they
Darned well please.

Goats eat flowers,
Goats eat fruits,
Small girls' pinafores and
Dad's old boots.

Spangled drongo lets his song go
From the mango tree;
Drongo can go round the mango
Catching grubs for tea.
You can have the grubs, old fellow,
Black and white and green and yellow;
Leave the fruit for me.

Max Fatchen

COUNTRY LUNCH

The basket is a big one, the billycan immense.
We carry them so carefully when getting through the fence.
The wind is full of hay smell and hawks patrol the sky,
    When we take the lunches out,
    Jeremy and I.

The harvester is whirring, it cuts the heads of wheat,
The dusty whirlwinds spiralling in columns through the heat.
There could be summer snakes about, or so our mother said.
    That's why we're walking warily
    And watching where we tread.

We've seen the paddock growing, for magical the rain,
With each stalk putting out its flags and nourishing its grain.
We've seen old farmers shaking heads because the season's dry;
    And we have been a part of it,
    Jeremy and I.

For country folks are worriers and though it's not a crime,
Yet parents seem (says Jeremy) to do it all the time . . .
The bills, the taxes and the kids and how the dams are low
    And so it sets us wondering
    Why people worry so.

But then it happens. Storms arrive and creeks go mad and flood
And there is gold in every drop and diamonds in the mud.
The neighbours call to celebrate, with sausage-rolls and tea
    And everything comes right again
    For Jeremy and me.

So now we take the lunches out. It's 'Hurry up, you kids.'
Undoing of the luncheon wraps and rattling billy-lids.
With half a dozen messages. You'll need to understand.
　　It's hurry, hurry, hurry,
　　With people on the land.

The grain trucks for the silo, the agent for the sheep,
'Now you remember, Jeremy. Your brain is half-asleep.
We'll get another drum of fuel. It won't do any harm.'
　　It's orders, orders, orders
　　When living on a farm.

'The steak and kidney pie is nice. Your mother's quite a cook.'
Our father's eyes are wandering with that slow farmer's look
That touches crop and heat-hazed land and plainly it will tell
　　He cares for me and Jeremy
　　And loves his earth as well.

We help him with the pannikins and clean the crusty plate.
The crop is ripe for harvesting. Tonight he's working late.
The summer's full of wonder (and steak and kidney pie)
　　When we take the lunch things home
　　Jeremy and I.

Doug MacLeod

BRENDA BAKER

Brenda Baker, quite ill-bred,
Used to cuddle fish in bed.
Tuna, trout and conger-eels,
Salmon, sole and sometimes seals.
Barracuda, bream and bass,
She cuddled them, until – alas!
One unforgotten Friday night
She slept with two piranhas,
And, being rather impolite,
They ate her best pyjamas!

Norman Lindsay

THE PENGUIN BOLD

To see the penguin out at sea,
And watch how he behaves,
Would prove that penguins cannot be
And never shall be slaves.
You haven't got a notion
How penguins brave the ocean,
And laugh with scorn at waves.

To see the penguin at his ease
Performing fearful larks
With stingarees of all degrees,
As well as whales and sharks;
The sight would quickly let you know
The great contempt that penguins show
For stingarees and sharks.

O see the penguin as he goes
A-turning Catherine wheels,
Without repose upon the nose
Of walruses and seals.
But bless your heart, a penguin feels
Supreme contempt for foolish seals,
While he never fails, where'er he goes,
To turn back-flaps on a walrus nose.

Margaret Mahy

PROMISES

If I had a needle, a needle,
I'd sew you a wonderful cake.
I'd crochet the cream,
I would stitch like a dream,
I would not make a single mistake.

I would hold it together with buttons,
Embroider it yellow and red,
But there could be hitches
With cakes made of stitches . . .
I'll knit you a sandwich instead.

Kate Walker

ELEPHANT'S LUNCH

CLARA Bear stared into her school bag and frowned.

'Are you sure you've given me enough to eat?' she asked her mother.

'Enough?' her mother cried. 'You've got four peanut butter sandwiches, six bananas, a piece of chocolate cake and an apple pie.'

'But I'll be at school *all* day,' said Clara, 'and I get awwwwfully hungry, especially in the afternoons.'

'Then don't eat everything in the morning,' her mother told her. 'Save something for later.'

'But I get awfully hungry in the mornings, too,' said Clara.

'You won't get hungry,' her mother said. 'You couldn't possibly get hungry. You've got enough lunch in there to fill an elephant. Now off you go.'

'All right,' said Clara Bear. 'If you say so.' And she kissed her mother goodbye and set off for school.

Half way there, Clara suddenly saw an elephant. He was standing on the other side of the railway line. He was big and grey and had little soft eyes.

Clara stopped and stared at him. The elephant stared back.

'Hello,' Clara said.

The elephant blinked and looked away along the tracks. Clara looked too. There was nothing coming.

'Are you waiting for a train?' she asked.

The elephant didn't answer.

'I waited for a train once,' said Clara, 'and it was late and I got awwwwwfully hungry. So hungry my tummy got angry and growled at me and made a pain. I hope your train isn't late because your tummy is much bigger than mine and you'll get an awfully big terrible pain.'

The elephant didn't say a word; his ears hung low.

Clara knew all about waiting for trains and how hungry that made you – more so than waiting for buses, or waiting for traffic lights to change. The elephant had to eat something. Clara opened her bag.

Elephants liked peanuts, every one knew that, so she took out one of her peanut butter sandwiches and offered it to him. But the elephant didn't take it; he just stared as blankly as before.

'Yummie, yummie, peanut butter!' Clara said and rubbed her tummy.

The elephant didn't seem to understand that she meant him to take it. So, to show him, she ate the first sandwich herself, making loud, enjoyable munching noises. Then she held out a second sandwich.

But again the elephant stared and didn't say a word.

Clara Bear ate the second sandwich, saying, 'Yummie yummie!' and rolling her eyes. But still the elephant didn't understand.

She ate the third one and licked her lips, 'Mmmmmm!'

The elephant raised his trunk and scratched his ear and simply looked away.

He wasn't a very smart elephant, Clara thought. 'If you don't eat this last, yummie, delicious, peanut butter sandwich,' said Clara, holding the fourth one out to him, 'I will.'

The elephant's trunk hung motionless.

'This is your last chance,' Clara said, and raised the sandwich over her mouth.

'And this is your second last chance.' She lowered it down.

'And this is your third last chance.' She put it in her wide-open mouth.

The elephant looked away. Clara closed her mouth and the sand-wich disappeared.

'You may not know this,' she said, 'but some trains are so late, they don't come at all. Imagine how hungry you'll get *then*!'

The elephant wiggled his ears slightly.

He's getting the message now, Clara thought. She delved into her bag and took out the six bananas, peeled them and laid them out on their skins for the elephant to take.

But the elephant looked away again. And now that the bananas were peeled they couldn't go back into the bag. They had to be eaten. Clara sat down and munched her way through all six of them.

'You're the fussiest animal I've ever met,' she said. 'And you'll be

sorry when your train doesn't come and you've got a big pain.'

She peered into her school bag again. 'I suppose you like chocolate cake?' she asked.

Silly question. Everybody in the whole world likes chocolate cake – especially chocolate cake with pink icing and coloured sprinkles. *sprinkl*

Clara Bear looked along the railway track. There was still no train in sight. 'All right,' she said at last, 'I'll share my cake with you.'

She broke the chocolate cake in half and placed one piece on the railway track for the elephant to take. She went to put the other piece back into her bag, but couldn't resist taking just one small bite. Then another. And then just one more. And then there was only one bite left and that wasn't worth putting away. So Clara popped it into her mouth and the cake was gone.

In the distance she heard a train coming. It had to be the elephant's train! He wouldn't go hungry after all.

Clara snatched up the piece of cake and backed well away from the railway line to watch the train come through. It pulled up and stood for a minute, then blew its whistle and moved off again, clicking and swaying away down the line.

When it had passed, the elephant was gone. And so was the other piece of chocolate cake. All that was left on Clara's paw was a smear of pink icing and a few coloured sprinkles. She'd gobbled it without thinking while watching the train pass through.

Now all she had for an entire day's lunch was one not-very-big apple pie.

'Oh dear, I'm going to get awfully hungry at school,' she thought. 'It'll be just like the time I waited for the train and it was late. My tummy will get angry and growl at me and make a pain.'

Clara acted quickly. She gobbled the apple pie to make her bag as light as possible, then ran all the way home.

Almost out of breath, she ran panting into the kitchen.

'Mummy, quick, I need some more lunch.' She held open her empty bag.

Her mother stared in disbelief. 'Clara, what happened to the lunch I gave you?'

'I ate it,' said Clara. 'I had to. You see, there was this elephant waiting for his train and . . .'

'So it was an elephant today,' her mother said.

'That's right,' said Clara, 'a big one.'

'Not a rhinoceros?' said her mother.

'No,' said Clara, 'that was yesterday that I met the rhinoceros.'

'And not a giraffe?'

'Don't you remember? That was the day before,' Clara smiled.

Mother Bear shook her head and started to make another lunch. 'I don't know where you put all this food, Clara,' she said.

'In my tummy, of course,' said Clara, 'so it won't growl at me and make a pain.'

'Well, I'm sorry to have to say this,' said her mother, a little annoyed, 'but Clara, you eat like an elephant.'

'That's not true!' said Clara. 'I happen to know that elephants don't eat very much at all.'

And, oddly enough, neither do camels, as Clara found out on her way to school the next day.

Edwin Miller

BISCUITS AND JAM

THERE was a young Irish girl named Molly O'Toole who lived alone with her mother.

One day Mother O'Toole said to her daughter, 'Molly,' she said, 'fetch the last bag of wool from the shed and take it to the market to sell. We are hard pressed and dearly need the money.'

Molly did as she was bade, and as she set off her mother wrapped some biscuits in a napkin and put them in a basket with a jar of blackberry jam. Mother O'Toole said to her daughter, she said, 'Here's a lunch for you, Molly. It isn't much, but it will see you through the day.'

Now the market was some way off, and Molly stepped quickly along with the sack of wool a'top her head and her lunch in a basket. After she had gone some distance she saw a spring in a shady nook, right near the road.

'Aha,' said Molly O'Toole, 'here is a fine place to eat my lunch of biscuits and jam.'

So she sat herself down in the shade, and had no sooner taken a biscuit and opened the jam than she saw that she had sat down in a fairy ring. Now everyone should know that a fairy ring is a ring of especially green grass, and if one of the wee folk finds you in the ring he'll have you in his power for a year and a day.

'Oh dear,' said Molly. She started to jump up, but just then she saw a man about eight inches tall in the grass. She knew she was found and had no chance of running away.

Instead, she quickly said, 'Hello there, and what's your name?'

'Me name is Hae-la-lag-ara,' said the little man boastfully; he was known far and wide for his mischief.

'My, that's such a big name for a boy,' said Molly, popping a biscuit loaded with jam into her mouth.

'I'm no boy, I'm one of the wee folk,' said Hae-la-lag-ara.

'Oh, surely you are just a boy,' said Molly. 'You are much too big for the wee folk.' And she popped another biscuit loaded with jam into her mouth.

'A boy?' asked Hae-la-lag-ara. 'Did you ever see a boy do *this?*'

And Hae-la-lag-ara spun around so fast that Molly could hardly see him. When he stopped, he was just half the size he was before.

'Now did you ever see a *boy* work such magic?' asked Hae-la-lag-ara.

'Well, no,' said Molly, 'but in my opinion you are still much too big for the wee folk.' And she popped another biscuit heaped with jam into her mouth.

'Is that so?' scoffed Hae-la-lag-ara. 'Well, did you ever see the like of this before?'

And Hae-la-lag-ara spun faster and faster. When he stopped he was only half the size, again.

'Now did you ever see such magic in your life?' asked Hae-la-lag-ara.

'Never,' said Molly O'Toole, 'but you must be a midget, for you are still much too large for the wee folk.' And she popped another biscuit loaded with jam into her mouth.

'A midget!' cried Hae-la-lag-ara. 'Did you ever see a midget do *this?*'

Hae-la-lag-ara was getting angry now; he spun around faster than ever. When he stopped he was only one inch tall.

'Now, me child, did you ever see a midget work magic like that?' asked Hae-la-lag-ara.

'No, I must confess I haven't,' said Molly, 'but I've always heard that the wee folk could fly.' And as she said this she popped the last two biscuits and all of the jam into her mouth.

'Fly?' sneered Hae-la-lag-ara. 'I'm as graceful as a swallow.' And he buzzed around Molly O'Toole's head like a pesky old gnat.

And as he flew, Molly suddenly reached up and clapped Hae-la-lag-ara into the empty jam-jar! She fastened the lid on tightly and threw the jar into the bushes. Then she picked up her sack of wool and her basket, and ran off down the road to market. She sold the wool, and was home in time for supper.

What happened to Hae-la-lag-ara, you ask?

Well, if you ever see a jar by the side of the road,

don't open it,

don't break it,

just leave it alone.

Margaret Mahy

THE FAT GHOST

Someone stole my
Tea and toast.
Could it be the
Breakfast ghost?

Ghosts who eat the
Breakfast scraps
Put on ghostly
Weight, perhaps.

Flibber! Flibber!
Flubber! Flubber!
Flobbing sound of
Flabbing rubber.

Thin ghost whisper
Quick and quiet:
'This ghost should be
On a diet.

'Where it feasted
Should have fasted.'
Flabber ghost is
Flabberghasted!

THE TWO HUNCHBACKS

ONCE there was a cheerful little hunchback, named Lusmore. He liked to keep busy, but had to take his time about it, what with his hump. One night, near midnight, he was resting his back against the wall of the ruined old Celtic fort of Knockgrafton. Sitting there, he heard the sweetest singing.

The sweetness of it, you'd not ever believe. There were hundreds of tiny, bell-clear voices, making harmony the like of which you'd never credit.

'*Da Luan, da Mort – Da Luan, da Mort!*' they sang.

(In the English, that's 'Monday, Tuesday – Monday, Tuesday!')

For a while, Lusmore listened, delighted and entranced by the beauty of the music. There'd come a pause at the end of the verse, then again:

'*Da Luan, da Mort – Da Luan, da Mort!*'

After a while it came to Lusmore that, though the melody was lovely beyond anything the like, perhaps the words could be bettered.

101

Next time the pause came, therefore, he piped up himself (and he'd as sweet a voice as any, had Lusmore, sweet as his nature).

'*Augus da Cadin!*' sang Lusmore, making it blend and fit, at his very best. (In the English, it meant 'And also Wednesday'.)

There was a surprised sort of silence, just for a moment. Then, with more joy than ever, clear and true, the singing swelled again, no harp music sweeter, and with Lusmore's words fitting in for a chorus:

'*Da Luan, da Mort . . . Augus da Cadin!*'

Then suddenly Lusmore was caught up in the air and whisked over the wall. Imagine, when he found himself in a bright, proud ballroom! The lights! There were crystal chandeliers all bright as day, gay flags and trimmings everywhere, and hundreds of Small Folk in their best silks and velvets, coloured bright as the rainbow, and dancing.

They clustered about Lusmore, patting and stroking him and saying, 'Aren't you the grand fellow, then, to give us this fine chorus to our song!'

Lusmore loved them all, and had never been so happy. Then he saw some, who looked important, whispering together. At this he worried just a wee trifle, for he'd heard how tricksy the Small Folk can be. But soon the leader stepped up to him and sang a special song:

'*Lusmore, Lusmore,*
Doubt not nor deplore!
For the hump which you bore
On your back is no more!'

Then there was a great bump, and Lusmore's hump slid from his shoulders. Well, it was true! The hump lay on the floor, the great lumpish load of it. Suddenly he felt tall and straight and light as a feather. He danced and jumped, so nimble he wondered he didn't hit his head on the sparkling ceiling. He laughed and skipped, and so did the Fairies, all about him, full of delight.

After a while he was worn out, what with the excitement of it and all. They sat him in a velvet chair, put cushions to his head and feet, and he dropped asleep.

Lusmore woke in his own bed. Had he dreamed the night? He felt his back, and it was straight and strong. He was also dressed in fine new clothes. His old ones no longer fitted him, d'you see, so the Fairies had dressed him in green velvet, from top to toe. Lusmore got up and ran about the village, telling everyone of his great good fortune. Why, folk came to hear of it from near and far.

There was a woman who trudged miles and miles to hear the way of it, for her best friend had a son with a hump. Jack Madden was his name.

'The Fairies will be sure to cure him!' cried Lusmore, and he told her just how it happened. (He was always anxious to share good fortune, and would do a good turn wherever he could.)

The woman returned to her village. Soon enough, she and her friend came back dragging a cart, with Jack Madden in it. (They were used always to fetch and carry for him.) As Lusmore had advised, they left him at the fort of the old Celts, Knockgrafton, at dusk, before moonrise. Jack Madden was a mean-natured fellow, but he'd like a cure well enough, and a new suit of clothes, for he was always looking for something for nothing.

Sure, about midnight, there came the sweet singing. And with Lusmore's chorus, too:

'*Da Luan, da Mort, da Luan, da Mort, da Luan da Mort . . . Augus da Cadin!*'

Jack Madden listened a while. He'd no ear for music, none whatever. Soon he was impatient and sick of it. He'd never let his mother sing around the cottage, or have children playing in the lane; they had to be quiet when he was about. A stupid song, thinks Jack Madden. He cut into it with his harsh voice, with no thought of the time or the tune.

'*Augus da Cadin, augus da Hena!*' he barked. (In the English, that's 'Yes, Wednesday and Thursday!')

The ruin opened and light streamed out – and an endless hoard of angry Fairies, all screaming and shouting, 'Who spoiled our tune? Who spoiled our tune?'

There was no bright ballroom for Jack Madden, at all. There was only a dark ruin, and they dragged him into it. Savage, flashing Small Folk clutched and clawed him. They propped him up somehow, and

the leader stepped up to him, and sang yet another song:

'*Jack Madden, Jack Madden!*
Your words come so bad in
The tune we feel glad in –
This castle you're had in
That your life we may sadden –
Wear two humps, Jack Madden!'

While he sang, a dozen of the strongest Fairies opened a side door and rolled out the hump that they'd taken from Lusmore. They lifted it up and clumped it down on top of Jack Madden's own hump. Then they pulled and kicked and buffeted him back onto the roadway. Suddenly the old ruin from the Dark Times was dark and deserted, silent as the grave.

In the morning, the two women came. They found Jack Madden there, more dead than alive.

Sure, the poor little fellow – if so you could call him – had a short life after that, and not at all a merry one.

Well, these old tales, you'll not be calling them lies, now. It would never do at all to so much as whisper that of the Small Folk.

Better watch your tongues, mind, and just think your own thoughts of the old tales.

A Celtic story
retold by Barbara Ker Wilson

THE FOX AND THE
GINGERBREAD MAN

MRS Farmer made a Gingerbread Man and gave him two currants for eyes. She baked him until he was brown and crispy, and put him aside to cool.

'My little son shall eat you bye and bye,' she told him.

The Gingerbread man did not like the sound of that at all. He did not want to be eaten by anyone! 'I will go out into the world to seek my fortune,' he decided; and as soon as Mrs Farmer turned her back, he hopped off the kitchen table and ran out of the door.

How wide was the world! Beyond the farmhouse lay a green hill that sloped down to a broad river. The Gingerbread Man ran helter-skelter down the hill on his thin crispy legs, but when he got to the bottom and saw the river he did not know what to do.

'How shall I ever get across?' he thought.

At that moment who should come by but the crafty Fox, with his pointed nose and red bushy tail. The Fox licked his lips when he saw the Gingerbread Man, and sniffed his spicy smell.

'Good day, Master Gingerbread! Am I right in thinking that you would like to get across this river?'

'Good day, Sir Fox,' the Gingerbread Man replied nervously, eyeing the Fox's sharp white teeth. 'I should indeed like to get to the other side of the river.'

'Then I will take you,' said the Fox, 'for I'm going that way myself.'

'I – er – I don't think that I can accept your offer, Sir Fox,' said the Gingerbread Man. 'I have an idea you want to eat me!'

The Fox pretended to be hurt by these words. 'Eat you? What could have given you such a strange idea? I have no intention of eating you. However, please yourself. If you do want to get across the river, hop on to the tip of my tail while I swim to the other side.'

Well, the Gingerbread Man thought he would surely be safe enough if he were that distance away from those sharp white teeth – so he hopped on to the Fox's red bushy tail.

The Fox stepped into the water. When they were a quarter of the way across, the water got deeper.

'You had better come on to my back, Gingerbread Man, for you are getting wet,' said the Fox.

The Gingerbread Man was indeed getting wet; his legs were beginning to feel quite soggy. So he moved on to the Fox's back.

When they were half-way across, the water got deeper still.

'You had better come and perch between my ears, Gingerbread Man, for you are getting wet,' said the Fox.

And the Gingerbread Man moved up and perched between the Fox's ears.

When they were three-quarters of the way across, the water was at its deepest, and was beginning to lap up over the fox's head. The Fox said, 'You had better come on to my nose, Gingerbread Man, for you are getting wet.'

The Gingerbread Man was indeed beginning to feel soggy all over, so he hopped on to the tip of the Fox's long, pointed nose.

What a foolish step that was! He had no sooner settled there than the Fox threw back his head and snapped him all up, every spicy crumb! My, how good he tasted, thought the fox.

And that is how the Gingerbread Man went out into the world and found his fortune.

A story from Burma
retold by Barbara Ker Wilson

THE MOUSE'S BRIDEGROOM

A FAMILY of mice once lived in a farmhouse: father, mother, and daughter. The two fond parents thought their daughter was the most beautiful mouse in the world, with her smooth brown coat, her long pink tail, and her delicate whiskers.

Another mouse, a bachelor, lived in the cattleshed in the farmyard. He was young and handsome, and he wanted to marry the beautiful Miss Mouse. But her parents did not consider him good enough for their daughter. They wanted her to marry the most powerful being on earth. So they told young Mister Mouse to go away.

What did Miss Mouse herself feel about this? She was very sad, for she had fallen in love with the young mouse from the cattleshed. Her brown coat lost its shine, and her delicate whiskers drooped.

Her parents, however, took no notice. Instead, they set out to find a bridegroom worthy of their daughter.

'Surely the Sun is the most powerful being of all,' said Father Mouse. 'He shines down upon the earth and ripens the corn in the fields. Let us ask the Sun to marry our daughter.'

So the two parent mice stood in the cornfield and asked the bright yellow Sun if he would marry their daughter. They were delighted when the Sun readily agreed to their proposal.

But no sooner had he said 'yes' than Mother Mouse felt a qualm of doubt. 'Ask him if he is really the most powerful being of all,' she urged Father Mouse.

So Father Mouse asked the Sun, 'Are you really the most powerful being of all?'

'No,' answered the Sun. 'The Rain is more powerful than I am. For when a Rain cloud covers the sky, I am blotted out completely.'

Even as he spoke, a great black Rain Cloud drifted across the Sun's face, hiding him from sight.

'In that case, I am very sorry, but you may not marry our daughter after all!' called Father Mouse, just before the sun disappeared from view.

Then he addressed the Rain Cloud. 'Tell me, Rain Cloud, are you in fact the most powerful being of all?'

The Rain Cloud scowled down at the two mice in the cornfield. 'No, I am not,' he replied. 'The Wind is more powerful than I am. For when the Wind blows, I am torn to shreds and scattered across the sky.'

'In that case, I am afraid you may not marry our daughter either,' said Father Mouse.

At that moment, the Wind began to blow. He swept across the sky, scattering the great black Rain Cloud in pieces.

'Oh Wind!' shouted Father Mouse. 'Is it true that you are the most powerful being of all?'

'No, not I!' blustered the Wind. 'Do you see that big grey Stone in the corner of the field? It is more powerful than I am. I cannot move it, however hard I blow.'

'In that case, I am afraid you may not marry our daughter either,' said Father Mouse.

Now the two mice went over to the big grey Stone that stood in one corner of the field.

'Are *you* the most powerful being of all?' Father Mouse asked the Stone.

'No, indeed,' answered the Stone. 'The red Bull is more powerful than I am. Every day he comes to sharpen his horns against my

109

surface, breaking off splinters of rock as he does so.'

'In that case, I am afraid you may not marry our daughter either,' said Father Mouse.

Next the two mice went to interview the red Bull, who stood tethered in his stall in the cattleshed.

'I think,' said Father Mouse, 'that you must be the most powerful being of all, and I have come to offer you my daughter.'

'You are wrong!' roared the Bull. 'This Rope that tethers me is more powerful than I am.'

'Oh,' said Father Mouse. 'In that case, I am afraid you may not marry our daughter after all.'

Now Mother Mouse spoke to the strong Rope that tethered the Bull. 'So you are the most powerful being of all!' she squeaked. 'Will you marry our daughter?'

'Much as I should like to marry your daughter,' replied the Rope, 'I must admit that there is one being even more powerful than I am, and that is the young Mouse who lives in this cattleshed. Every night, as the Bull stands tethered in his stall, this Mouse comes to gnaw at me with his sharp teeth. In time he will gnaw right through me, and I will break.'

'Well!' said Father Mouse. And, 'Well, well!' exclaimed Mother Mouse. They looked at each other shamefacedly. Then they sought out the handsome young bachelor Mouse who lived in the cattleshed, and begged him to marry their daughter after all.

Young Mister Mouse was very surprised, and quite overjoyed. As for Miss Mouse, when she heard the good news that she was to marry the bridegroom of her own choice after all, her coat at once regained its shine, and she preened her delicate whiskers prettily. So the two mice were married, and lived happily every after.

MUSHKIL GUSHA

THIS is a story to be told of a Thursday evening, over a handful of dates.

Well, there was once a poor woodcutter who lived with his daughter, Fathima, at the edge of the forest. He'd be up before the sun, pray towards Mecca, then go into the forest and cut a bundle of wood. He'd return to the hut to eat a bowl of curds, then take his wood to the town and sell it. With luck, he'd have money, then, to buy a flap of bread and perhaps some tabouli, or a bit of goat's meat for a kebab. Home he'd go, and he and his daughter would eat.

One day, when he was home very late, with only bread and tabouli, Fathima said, 'Father, I wish we could have some nicer food, and different. Some folk have rose candy, and some have walnuts and honey.'

It grieved the woodcutter to know that he could not give his child all. On thinking deeply, he said, 'Fathima, tomorrow I will get up much earlier. I will go far, and cut a great, great load of wood. I will, even so, be early into the town, and sell my huge load for much money. With it, you shall feast.'

111

Next morning he rose while it was still dark and Fathima was sleeping soundly. He went far into the forest and finally struggled home with an enormous load. He knocked on the hut door, crying, 'Fathima, let me in! I must have a little food and water, before I go to the town.'

But the door remained locked. Fathima had woken late, quite forgetting about her talk with her father. She'd eaten the curds and gone off to the village, locking the door behind her.

Hungry and thirsty, the woodcutter fell asleep with his head on the load of wood. He soon woke. It was past time to go to the town, so he trudged back to the forest, cut more wood, and struggled home with another load. Now he was terribly hungry and thirsty, and it was dark.

'Fathima, Fathima!' he called, knocking on the door. But Fathima had come home, wondered why her father wasn't there, then had eaten the last of the tabouli, locked the door, and gone to her bed. She was sleeping sweetly.

The woodcutter fell into a doze, but he was so cold, hungry and thirsty that he soon woke. He did not know what to do. So he began to tell himself his own tale of misfortune.

A sudden voice stopped him: 'Woodcutter!' Yet there was nobody there. The voice called again: 'Woodcutter! You can hear me! Go up the stairs!'

'What stairs?' asked the woodcutter – of nobody. Yet he did as the voice bade him. As he raised his foot, he felt a step beneath it – and another and another. Up he went, until he came into a bright desert land, covered in pebbles. The voice spoke on: 'Carry as many pebbles as you can, and return down the stairs.'

So the Woodcutter filled his pockets and his sleeves and his turban with bright pebbles, and walked confidently down the dark stairs, with never a stumble. Lo! He was at his door!

'Woodcutter!' called the voice. 'You have been saved by Mushkil Gusha, the Solver of Problems. All will go well with you now, as long as you tell your story over a handful of dates, with some needy person, every Thursday evening!'

It was Thursday now. The woodcutter knocked on his door and Fathima opened it. He told her all that had happened. They put the great pile of pebbles under the window, and Fathima and her father had fresh curds and a long drink of sweet water, and then a little buttermilk that she had saved.

Refreshed, the woodcutter carried his double load of wood into the

town. He told his story to all, and sold his wood for much money. He bought dates, and shared them with the poor in the market place. Then he took home all kinds of good food to Fathima. He took red pickled cabbage and olives and rose candy and honey cakes with walnuts and many other good things. Such a meal she ate!

That night, neighbours knocked on the woodcutter's door.

'We have no light, will you lend us your lamps?' they said.

The pebbles from the bright desert land were shining through the window in rainbow colours. Fathima and the woodcutter covered them in a hurry, and told the neighbours: 'Alas, we are sorry, but the oil is used up.' The neighbours were not surprised, and soon went home.

In the morning, the woodcutter found that the pebbles had turned into priceless jewels: diamonds, rubies, emeralds and sapphires. One by one, he took them to this city and that, and sold them for a fortune.

Fathima lived like a princess. Then the woodcutter built a shining palace of a home for her, close to the palace of the king.

The king had a daughter, and she and Fathima became firm friends. The woodcutter was so interested in his fine castle and fine food, however, that a Thursday came, and he never noticed; nor did he see any poor person to give dates to, or to hear his story.

The next day, the Princess lost her necklace, and thought that Fathima must have stolen it. She had her father throw the woodcutter into prison, and send Fathima to an orphanage.

After a while in prison, as was the custom, the woodcutter was taken out and chained in the market place with a begging bowl. How he missed his hut in the forest now!

One day, as some kind person tossed a coin into his begging bowl, he remembered that it was Thursday.

'Your Graciousness, your Excellency!' he cried. 'The coin is no use to me, but your kindness is! Please take the coin and buy a few dates, and share them with me!'

This the stranger did. As they ate the dates, the woodcutter told his story, and how he had been helped by Mushkil Gusha.

The very next day, the Princess found her necklace! She ran to her father, begging him to bring back the woodcutter and Fathima.

Soon all was restored to the woodcutter. He and Fathima lived happily for ever after, and you can be sure that he never forgot Mushkil Gusha, Solver of Problems, or missed a Thursday.

What's more, the stranger of the market place, he also remembered Mushkil Gusha. Of a Thursday evening, he would share dates with the poor, and tell his story, and listen to theirs.

*A story from Burma
retold by Barbara Ker Wilson*

THE CROW AND THE WREN

ONE day, Crow seized Wren in his claws. 'I am going to eat you, little Wren!' he said.

'Oh no! Who will look after my dear little fledgling when I am gone?' cried the Wren pitifully.

When the Crow heard this, he paused. The Wren must be old and tough, he thought, but her fledgling will be young and tender. So he said to the Wren, 'I will let you go on condition that you bring your little fledgling to me on the seventh day from now.'

'I promise! I promise!' cheeped the Wren.

And the Crow let her go.

On the seventh day he came to the Wren's nest and demanded her fledgling.

'Before you eat my fledgling, you must clean your dirty beak,' the Wren told him. 'Let me see you wash it in some water.'

'Very well,' said the Crow, 'I will go and fetch some water.'

He spread his wings and flew away. Soon he came to a stream, and called out in his harsh voice:

116

'Water, water, come with me
To wash my beak
To eat the little Wren!'

'How can I come with you unless you bring a pot to carry me in?' gurgled the water.

So the Crow spread his wings again and flew away to find a pot. Presently he saw one lying in the grass, and swooped to pick it up.

'Pot, pot, come with me
To hold the water
To wash my beak
To eat the little Wren!' he called.

'I would come with you,' replied the Pot, 'but there is a hole in my side, and the water would leak out. You will have to get some mud to mend the hole.'

The Crow flew off once more, and alighted beside a pool of mud.

'Mud, mud, come with me
To mend the pot
To hold the water
To wash my beak
To eat the little Wren!'

'I would come with you,' answered the Mud, 'but the hot sun has made me hard and dry. You must ask the Buffalo to come and wallow here.'

So the Crow flew off to look for the Buffalo. Not far away he found him lying on the ground. The Crow hopped up to him and said:

'Buffalo, buffalo, come with me
To wallow in the mud
To mend the pot
To hold the water
To wash my beak
To eat the little Wren!'

'I would come with you,' said the Buffalo, 'but I am weak from hunger. I have not the strength to walk to the pool of mud. Go and get me some grass to eat. Then I will come.'

The Crow left the Buffalo and flew to a clump of grass.

'*Grass, grass, come with me*
To feed the Buffalo
To wallow in the mud
To mend the pot
To hold the water
To wash my beak
To eat the little Wren!'

'I would come with you,' said the Grass, 'but the Buffalo is such a large animal that he needs a great deal to eat, more than I can provide at the moment. However, if you can find me more land, I will spread out until there is enough of me to satisfy the Buffalo.'

The Crow flew away yet again, and circled above a forest of trees.

'*Land, land, come with me*
To grow the grass
To feed the Buffalo
To wallow in the mud
To mend the pot
To hold the water
To wash my beak
To eat the little Wren!'

'I would come with you,' answered the Land, 'but, as you can see, I am covered with trees. The grass cannot grow on me until the trees have gone.'

So the Crow called to the trees:

'*Trees, trees, go away*
To clear the land
To grow the grass
To feed the Buffalo
To wallow in the mud
To mend the pot
To hold the water
To wash my beak
To eat the little Wren!'

'We would go away,' the Trees replied, rustling their branches,

119

'but we cannot move. Our roots are held firmly in the earth. Only fire could move us from the land.'

Once more the Crow spread his wings and flew away. In a village he found a fire.

> *'Fire, fire, come with me*
> *To move the trees*
> *To clear the land*
> *To grow the grass*
> *To feed the Buffalo*
> *To wallow in the mud*
> *To mend the pot*
> *To hold the water*
> *To wash my beak*
> *To eat the little Wren!'*

'Yes, I will come with you!' crackled the Fire, and it leapt up to meet him. At last! thought the wicked Crow. Now I will be able to eat that juicy little wren for my dinner after all! But alas, the orange and yellow flames were so fierce that they burnt the Crow until there was nothing left of him. And so – the trees did not move, the land was not cleared, the grass did not grow, the Buffalo stayed hungry, the mud remained hard, the hole in the pot was not mended, the water stayed where it was, and the Crow did not eat the little Wren after all.

A story from Papua New Guinea
retold by Robin Anderson

SINABOUDA LILY

O N the western side of Kwato Island, in Papua New Guinea, lived a little girl with her mother, father and two brothers. Her name was Sinabouda Lily.

Right beside the water, near their house, grew a big bodilla nut tree. From one of its branches hung a loop of thick, green vine. It made a wonderful swing for the little girl. People from her village called her Sinabouda Lily, the swing girl.

Every morning, Sinabouda Lily ran down to the beach and climbed onto her swing. Day after day she swung back and forth, going higher and higher and further and further, until she almost reached the nearby island of Bonarurahilihili.

Sinabouda Lily was very happy on her swing, but her mother warned her, 'You must be careful, Sinabouda Lily. On the island of Bonarurahilihili lives the wicked witch Sinawakelakela Tanotano, and she loves to eat children!'

'Oh Mother, I saw the witch yesterday. I told her she couldn't hurt me as long as my father and brothers are here to protect me. But the witch dared me to lean out further, and when I laughed, she shook her fist and said, "One day I will catch you".'

Not long after that, the family had to go out across the bay on a fishing trip. Sinabouda Lily begged to be allowed to stay at home and spend the day on her swing.

Her mother wasn't happy to leave her, but her father said she would be quite safe. He left her a big bunch of ripe bananas over which he had worked a magic spell. He told Sinabouda Lily that if she was frightened, or in any trouble, she had only to talk to the bananas, and he would hear her and answer. He hung the bananas on a branch of the bodilla nut tree.

The rest of the family set out across the bay in their canoe, leaving Sinabouda Lily swinging happily back and forth on her swing. And as she swung, she ate bananas from the bunch and threw the skins into the sea.

Sinabouda Lily felt quite safe with the magic bananas, but her father had forgotten to tell her one very important thing. If she ate the bananas and threw away the skins, the magic spell would not work.

Across on the island of Bonarurahilihili, the wicked witch Sina-wakelakela Tanotano hid and watched as the family set out in their canoe. She crept down to the beach and, when she saw the magic banana skins, she rushed to the water's edge to collect them.

High up on her swing, Sinabouda Lily saw the witch collecting the banana skins.

The wicked witch must be very hungry to collect skins to eat, she thought. And she swung out closer to the island to get a better look.

Suddenly the witch reached out and tried to grab Sinabouda Lily. The little girl screamed, and from the bunch of bananas hanging in the tree came the voice of her father: 'Do not be afraid, my child, I am here.'

When the wicked witch heard the father's voice, she ran away.

Slowly the day passed and the sun was low in the sky.

Soon my family will return with all their fish, thought Sinabouda Lily. She took the last banana from the bunch and threw the stalk into the sea. Then she climbed back onto her swing to wait for her family to come home. And the banana stalk floated out to sea.

But the wicked witch had been hiding and watching. When she saw

Sinabouda Lily eat the last banana and throw the stalk into the sea, she jumped out of her hiding place and grabbed the little girl as she swung out towards the island.

'Ha, ha!' she cried, 'I have caught you at last. I'll soon have you in my cooking pot!'

Sinabouda Lily screamed, 'Mother! Father! Brothers!' but it was no use. There was no answering voice from her father.

The wicked witch tied her up, carried her along the beach and put her in a cooking pot.

Far out in the bay, the family saw the banana stalk floating on the water. They knew at once that something was wrong and they quickly turned their canoe and headed straight for the island of Bonarurahili-hili.

Just as they landed, they saw the wicked witch struggling up the beach with a load of firewood for her cooking pot. She was bent nearly double under the weight of the wood.

Sinabouda Lily's father rushed at the witch and struck her down. As she fell to the ground and died, the firewood spilled out behind her and she turned into a rock.

And if you go to that beach on the island of Bonarurahilihili, near Kwato, you can still see the rock that is all that remains of the wicked witch Sinawakelakela Tanotano.

Chris Wallace-Crabbe

EMUS

It is
particularly
the particular way
they come
stepping
warily
along the path
in dark
wrinkled
stockings
and shabby
mini fur coats,
their weaving
Donald Duck
heads
ready
to dip
and snatch
your ice cream
that appeals;
that,
and the way
they browse dumbly brown
in cattle-paddocks.

A. B. Paterson

OLD MAN PLATYPUS

Far from the trouble and toil of town,
Where the reed-beds sweep and shiver,
Look at a fragment of velvet brown –
Old Man Platypus drifting down,
Drifting along the river.

And he plays and dives in the river bends
In a style that is most elusive;
With few relations and fewer friends,
For Old Man Platypus descends
From a family most exclusive.

He shares his burrow beneath the bank
With his wife and his son and daughter
At the roots of the reeds and the grasses rank;
And the bubbles show where our hero sank
To its entrance under water.

Safe in their burrow below the falls
They live in a world of wonder,
Where no one visits and no one calls,
They sleep like little brown billiard balls
With their beaks tucked neatly under.

And he talks in a deep unfriendly growl
As he goes on his journey lonely;
For he's no relation to fish nor fowl,
Nor to bird nor beast, nor to horned owl;
In fact, he's the one and only!

Margaret Mahy

A WITCH POEM

The witch my sister from over the sea
Wonderful presents has sent to me.
A whistle to blow and a bell to ring,
Silver ropes for a shining swing,
A golden lion that will play and purr,
Dancing slippers of silver fur,
And, sharp as a needle, bright as a pin,
A mouse that plays on the violin.

Sally Farrell Odgers

MOONSTRUCK!

If you met Lucan's family,
you'd reckon they were strange.
When moonlight caught them off their guard
they'd undergo a change.
Their house had bricked up windows,
and hardly any doors.
They'd darkened all the ceilings,
and blackened all the floors.
They couldn't simply wander off,
in case the sun went down.
Not one of them had been to school –
nor even into town.
Little Lucan sighed a lot
and wished that he could go,
but relatives would frown
and mutter, 'No, no, no!'
Little Lucan didn't care
if he was changed about.
He'd rather be another shape –
if that would get him out.
And so he made a run for it
one clear and chilly day.
Uncle Bradley chased him back,
but lingered on the way.
The sun slid down, up came the moon,
then someone gave a squawk –
and there, where Uncle Brad had been,
young Lucan saw a hawk!
His mum and dad rushed out to have

a disbelieving look.
The moon transformed them instantly
to rooster and to chook!
'What bothers me,' wailed Auntie Bess
of feathered Uncle Brad,
'is what if he forgets himself
and eats your mum and dad?'
The family (sad, naturally)
debated what to do,
but Little Lucan saw
a possibility or two.
The indoor life would irk him less
if he could have a pet.
But though he asked persistently,
he hadn't got one yet.
So, silently he sat and thought,
his eye on toothless Gran,
of how he longed to have a dog.
And then he hatched a plan.
He sneaked into his Granny's room
where, with his pocket knife,
he sawed into the ceiling
until he'd cut a slice.
He yelled at Gran to come and see,
then, as the moon came up,
he pushed the piece of ceiling out –
Ah! Soon he'd have his pup!
Poor Gran, transfigured by the moon,
fell backwards into bed,

but Lucan hadn't got his dog –
he had a cow instead!
His subsequent attempt went wrong –
he got a Grandpa bird.
And after that, an elephant –
which was a bit absurd.
So, one by one, the family
turned into other things,
and Lucan's place was always full
of feet and fur and wings.
Apart from Little Lucan,
there was only Auntie Kate.
All the rest had met the moon
and changed their outward shape.
Little Lucan thought he'd try
to make an auntly mouse.
He planned to trap his relative
that night, outside the house.
He locked her out but later on
she gave a toothy grin.
Now Auntie was a crocodile,
and Auntie *swallowed* him!
She said, '*Dear* little Lucan,'
as she gulped her nephew down.
'He'll always stay the shape he is –
the moon can't get him now!'

Morris Lurie

THE TALKING BOW TIE

THAT evening, Mr Baxter brought home a brand-new bow tie.

'Oh, very lovely!' said Mrs Baxter, and it was.

It was the boldest bright yellow with the biggest purple spots, and it looked very happy and gay.

'I thought I'd wear it tonight,' said Mr Baxter.

Mr and Mrs Baxter were going out to dinner.

So, Mr Baxter had a shower, and then he put on a nice clean white shirt (and his underwear and trousers and shoes and socks, too, of course), and then he popped himself in front of the big mirror in the bathroom and put on the brand-new bow tie.

'Oh, yes indeed!' he said, giving it a little straighten this way and that. 'Very smart!'

'Very smart?' said the bow tie.

'What?' said Mr Baxter.

'You don't look very smart,' said the bow tie. 'You look ridiculous.'

'I beg your pardon?' said Mr Baxter.

'You are one of the most ridiculous-looking people I have ever seen,' said the bow tie.

'Mary!' cried Mr Baxter, running out of the bathroom. 'Mary! This bow tie just spoke to me! It said I looked ridiculous!'

Mrs Baxter was busy in the kitchen preparing dinner for the children, and she didn't really hear what Mr Baxter said.

'Well, wear something else, dear,' she said, serving up the children's lamb chops.

'What?' said Mr Baxter. 'Oh. All right.'

And he took off the bow tie and put on his favourite pale blue tie instead, which was very nice and had no spots at all.

The next morning, when she was doing the cleaning, Mrs Baxter saw the brand-new bow tie lying on the dressing table, where Mr Baxter had dropped it.

'Oh, how pretty!' she said, not remembering a single thing about it. She picked it up and held it to her hair. 'I think it suits me,' she said. 'Yes, I think I'll wear it this afternoon when I go shopping.'

'Your nose is too long,' said the bow tie.

'I beg your pardon?' said Mrs Baxter.

'It looks like a sausage,' said the bow tie. 'And your eyes are too small, too. They look like shrivelled raisins.'

'What?' said Mrs Baxter.

'In fact,' said the bow tie, 'your face is one of the silliest faces I have ever seen.'

'Oh, you horrid thing!' cried Mrs Baxter, and she flung the bow tie as far away as she could, out into the hall.

Now, the Baxters had two children, a boy and a girl. The boy's name was Michael. And at four o'clock that afternoon he came home, as usual, from school.

'Hi!' he called. 'Anyone home?'

There was a note on the kitchen table.

Gone to have my hair done, it said. *Be back soon.*
There are some lovely new apples in the fruit bowl.
   Love, Mother.

So, Michael took an apple and started to munch it, and then he saw the brand-new bow tie lying on the floor in the hall.

'Hey, what a great bow tie!' he said, picking it up. 'I think I'll wear it to school tomorrow!'

'Don't be ridiculous,' said the bow tie.

'What?' said Michael. 'Who said that?'

'Your head's like a rubbish tin with the lid jammed on crooked,' said the bow tie.

'Get out of it!' said Michael.

'And the rest of you doesn't look too hot, either, if you want to know the truth,' said the bow tie.

'I don't need this!' cried Michael, and he threw the bow tie down and went for a long, long ride on his bike.

Then Michael's sister came home. Her name was Suzie. She picked the bow tie up at once.

'Oh, how gorgeous!' she said.

'But you're not,' said the bow tie.

'Did you say something?' said Suzie.

'You've got a face like a pickled pillow,' said the bow tie. 'And your ears look like jug handles poking out of your head.'

'Well, I don't like you either,' said Suzie, and she threw the bow tie over her shoulder and went off to her room to read a good book.

Now, the Baxters had a dog, a very floppy and friendly dog, and his name was Ebenezer.

'I know,' said Mrs Baxter when she came home. 'I'll give that bow tie to Ebenezer. It wouldn't dare say anything to him.'

And she tied the bow tie very carefully around Ebenezer's neck.

'Yes,' she said. 'Quite nice.'

'What a smelly dog,' said the bow tie. 'He smells like an over-cooked cabbage. He smells like a pair of old socks.'

'Woof!' cried Ebenezer, and he tore off the bow tie and ran under the sofa in the front room and wouldn't come out all night.

The last member of the Baxter family to try the bow tie was the family cat. She was small and white and fluffy and her name was Daphne, and I don't know how she came to wear the bow tie, but she did.

'What a silly looking cat,' said the bow tie. 'You look like a mouldy cheese. You look like a cross-eyed mop.'

'Miaow!' cried Daphne, and she snatched off the bow tie and flew straight up the tallest tree in the garden and absolutely refused to come down, even for her supper.

'This has gone on quite long enough!' said Mr Baxter. 'That bow tie is totally terrible! It has insulted everyone! It must be taught a lesson at once! There is only one thing to do!'

And he put it in the refrigerator, in the freezer part, next to the fish fingers, and he left it there for three whole days and nights.

And when he took it out, believe you me, that talking bow tie never spoke again.

Norman Lindsay

THE TALE OF A DESPICABLE PUDDIN' THIEF

A puddin' thief, as I've heard tell,
　　Quite lost to noble feeling,
Spent all his days, and nights as well,
　　In constant puddin'-stealing.

He stole them here, he stole them there,
　　He knew no moderation;
He stole the coarse, he stole the rare,
　　He stole without cessation.

He stole the steak-and-kidney stew
　　That housewives in a rage hid;
He stole the infants' Puddin' too,
　　The Puddin' of the aged.

He lived that Puddin's he might lure,
　　Into his clutches stealthy;
He stole the Puddin' of the poor,
　　The Puddin' of the wealthy.

This evil wight went forth one night
　　Intent on puddin'-stealing,
When he beheld a hidden light
　　A secret room revealing.

Within he saw a fearful man,
　　With eyes like coals a-glowing,
Whose frightful whiskers over-ran
　　His face, like weeds a-blowing;

And there this fearful, frightful man,
    A sight to set you quaking,
With pot and pan and curse and ban,
    Began a puddin' making.

Twas made of buns and boiling oil,
    A carrot and some nails-O!
A lobster's claws, the knobs off doors,
    An onion and some snails-O!

A pound of fat, an old man rat,
    A pint of kerosene-O!
A box of tacks, some cobbler's wax,
    Some gum and glycerine-O!

Gunpowder too, a hob-nailed shoe,
    He stirred into his pottage;
Some Irish stew, a pound of glue,
    A high explosive sausage.

The deed was done, that frightful one,
    With glare of vulture famished,
Blew out the light, and in the night
    Gave several howls, and vanished.

Our thieving lout, ensconced without,
    Came through the window slinking;
He grabbed the pot and on the spot
    Began to eat like winking.

He ate the lot, this guzzling sot –
    Such appetite amazes –
Until those high explosives wrought
Within his tum a loud report,
    And blew him all to blazes.

For him who steals ill-gotten meals
    Our moral is a good un.
We hope he feels that it reveals
    The danger he is stood in
Who steals a high explosive bomb,
    Mistaking it for Puddin'.

Max Fatchen

WRY RHYMES

Pussycat, pussycat, where have you been,
Licking your lips with your whiskers so clean?
Pussycat, pussycat, purring and pudgy,
Pussycat, pussycat – *where is our budgie?*

When Old Mother Hubbard
Went to the cupboard
Her dog for a morsel would beg.
'Not a scrap can be found,'
She explained to her hound
So he bit the poor dear on the leg.

A cautionary tale
by Nan McNab

GREEDY GREGORY'S TOOTH

GREEDY Gregory's tooth had been loose for days. At school, while he was meant to be learning his tables, Greedy Gregory pushed at the tooth with his tongue. When he ate his lunch he would bite down hard on his choo-choo bar, hoping that the tooth would come out. It did get stuck in a lump of Jersey toffee once, but Greedy Gregory was too scared to tug it out – he had to wait half an hour for the toffee to dissolve.

Walking home from school, he twisted the tooth back and forth with his dirty fingers but, even though it was only hanging by a thread, it still wouldn't come out.

Then, late one afternoon, his sister caught him by surprise with a kung-fu kick to the jaw. He was just about to counter-attack when he felt the tooth – it was lying on his tongue, just behind his bottom teeth, and there was a big spongy lump where his tooth used to be.

'Maaam, Daaad!' he yelled.

'You sook!' said his little sister. 'I hardly touched you . . .'

But Greedy Gregory pushed past her and ran into the kitchen.

'Mum! Dad! Look at me toof. What a beauty!'

Greedy Gregory's dad took down a glass and filled it up with water. 'Put your tooth in that,' he said, 'and we'll see what the tooth fairy brings you tonight.'

Greedy Gregory dropped the tooth into the glass of water and held it up to the light. The tooth looked even bigger through the glass.

'A toof like that must be worth at least a dollar,' said Greedy Gregory.

'Don't be funny,' said his dad. 'You'll be lucky to get five cents for it – it's got a great big hole in it. Not to mention the colour.'

Greedy Gregory scowled at his dad. 'That toof fairy had better give me a dollar or I'll smash 'er,' he said, and he went off to the bathroom to count the rest of his teeth. His sister followed him and watched while he stood in front of the mirror and opened his mouth wide. It was not a pretty sight. All his teeth were green or grey, and bits of his lunch were still stuck in the gaps.

'Un, ooo, eee, or, ive, ix . . .' Greedy Gregory counted all his teeth, top and bottom – incisors, canine teeth and molars – then he multiplied by a dollar (the one-times table was the only one he could remember).

'I'll be rich!' he cried. 'Twenty dollars! Think of all the lollies I can buy with twenty dollars!' And he counted his teeth all over again, just to be sure.

'You won't get a dollar a tooth for those horrible green things,' said his sister, and marched off to practise her karate.

'Just you wait and see,' he yelled. 'If I don't get a dollar a toof, that fairy'd better watch out,' and he pulled his most ferocious face.

That night, Greedy Gregory went to bed extra early to wait for the tooth fairy. He put the glass of water on his bedside table and stared at the tooth. It did look a bit green in the lamplight. There was a dark brown hole in the side, but Greedy Gregory was sure it was worth more than five cents. It was such a *big* tooth, and besides, it was *his*. I'll stay awake till the toof fairy comes, he thought, and if she tries to leave me anything less than a dollar I'll . . . *yawn*. Greedy Gregory's eyes began to close, and his head sank on to his chest.

'*Ping!*' Something long and hard and springy landed on Gregory's head.

'Uh – what . . . ?' Greedy Gregory blinked. There was a funny blue light in the room. He rubbed his eyes.

'I said *ping!*'

Gregory looked up, and up, and up. The biggest tooth fairy he had ever seen was standing beside his bed, whacking him on the head with her wand.

'Are you Greedy Gregory?' she snapped.

'Yes I am.'

'And is this your tooth?'

'Yes it is,' said Greedy Gregory.

'Right,' said the fairy, tucking her wand under her arm and plonking herself down on the bed. 'How much do you want for it?'

Gregory wished she'd move over a bit – she was squashing his legs. His knees felt as if they might bend back the wrong way at any moment.

'Come on – don't muck about,' said the fairy. 'Do you know how many kids I have to see tonight?'

'I want a dollar,' said Greedy Gregory.

'Nothing doing,' said the fairy. 'The going rate is five cents.'

'Not for Gregory Grabham's teef,' he replied firmly.

'Oh, indeed? Pardon me,' said the fairy. 'I thought we were talking about this nasty green object.' The fairy prodded the tooth with her wand. 'Gregory Grabham's *teeth*,' she added, 'are a different matter.' And she began to do some quick calculations.

Greedy Gregory leant back on his pillow and watched the fairy filling in some figures in a little book. Fairies are all the same, he thought smugly, treat them tough and they give you what you want.

'This is the first tooth you've ever lost?' asked the fairy.

'Yes.'

'So, counting this tooth, you've got twenty teeth altogether?'

'That's right,' said Gregory. The fairy was obviously no fool – she

knew how much she'd have to pay for a Gregory Grabham tooth. He began to imagine the sweets and ice creams he'd be able to buy tomorrow.

'Right,' said the fairy, under her breath. 'Twenty teeth at five cents a tooth makes a dollar.' (The fairy knew her five-times tables back to front.)

Greedy Gregory was so busy thinking of food that he only heard the last bit: '. . . a tooth makes a dollar'.

'That's right,' he said firmly. 'I'll take nothing less than a dollar.'

'All right,' said the fairy, 'a dollar it is. Sign here.' And she held out the book for Gregory to sign with a special magic pencil that wrote everything in triplicate.

Greedy Gregory was so eager to get his dollar that he signed straight away without reading a word of the contract.

'Done!' said the fairy, shutting the book with a bang. 'Now, open your mouth.'

'What?' cried Gregory.

'Open your mouth!' said the fairy. 'Don't muck about.'

'Why should I?' said Greedy Gregory.

The fairy was getting impatient, and her face was getting redder and redder. 'Look,' she said, 'we made a deal. You get your dollar and I get your teeth.'

'My *what?*' squeaked Gregory.

'Your teeth, dumbskull. Now open your mouth.'

Greedy Gregory went very pale. 'But . . . but . . .' he stammered, 'I thought it was a dollar a toof.'

'Don't be wet,' said the fairy. 'A dollar for *that*! Look at it.' She picked the tooth up gingerly between her finger and thumb, and held it under Gregory's nose. 'It's *green!*' she snapped. 'It hasn't been cleaned for *months*! And it's got a big ugly *hole* in one side. What use is a tooth like that?'

Greedy Gregory stared at his tooth. It didn't look too good, jammed between the fairy's big freckly fingers. A drop of dirty water fell off the end of the tooth and soaked into the sheet. Gregory began to cry.

143

'Now look here,' said the fairy, 'no crying – it was all fair and square. You want a dollar, right? At five cents a tooth, multiplied by twenty teeth, you get a dollar. Now I can't say fairer than that.'

Gregory wished he'd practised his five-times tables. His teacher was right – you never knew when you might need them.

The fairy reached into a bag she had slung over her back and pulled out an enormous pair of pliers. 'Come on now,' she said gruffly, 'I can't muck around all night.'

Greedy Gregory felt sick. 'I don't want a dollar,' he snivelled, staring at the huge pliers. 'I want to keep my teef!'

The fairy waved the pliers at Gregory. 'Look, kid – we made a deal and you signed it fair and square.'

'But I want to un-make it,' sobbed Gregory.

'Can't un-make a deal,' said the fairy sternly. 'All you can do is make a new one.'

'Yes! Yes!' he cried. 'Anything.'

The fairy pulled out another book and flipped through the pages. 'Well,' she said, 'you haven't got much to offer me – unless your teeth improve a bit. Perhaps Form CT.20 might do the trick.'

Greedy Gregory wiped his eyes and peered at the form. This time he read every word – even the fine print at the bottom of the page. Here is what it said:

'I, ... , do solemnly swear to take good care of all my teeth, to visit the dentist every six months, and to brush my teeth after every meal. Signed .... '

And in the small print at the bottom:

'I also promise not to eat too many lollies or ice creams or sweet biscuits.'

Gregory signed.

Next morning, Gregory woke late. His eyes were all puffy and he felt awful. He ran his tongue over this teeth. Thank goodness – they were all there, just as furry and dirty as they were last night. He raced into the bathroom and grabbed a toothbrush.

'Did you look in your tooth glass?' asked his mum as he scrubbed away at his teeth. 'The tooth fairy left you something.'

Gregory walked slowly back into his room. There on the sheet was the dirty mark where the tooth fairy had dropped a little water the night before. Greedy Gregory hardly dared to look in the glass. What if there were a dollar coin at the bottom – would she come back another night with her pliers and pull out all his teeth?

But there at the bottom of the glass was a shiny silver five-cent coin.

'Look, Mum,' said Gregory, 'five cents!' And he gave his mother a big, white, gleaming smile.

Spike Milligan

THREE SOLDIERS

Soldier Freddy
was never ready,
But! Soldier Neddy,
unlike Freddy
Was always ready
and steady.
That's why,
when Soldier Neddy
Is-outside-Buckingham-Palace-on guard-in-the-
pouring-wind-and-rain-
being-steady-and-ready,
Freddy –
is home in beddy.

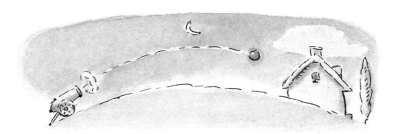

There was a young soldier called Edser
When wanted was always in bed sir.
One morning at one
They fired a gun
And Edser, in bed sir, was dead sir.

Jenny Wagner

PARBURY'S GHOST

AMARANTHUS knew all about ghosts. On nights when they showed ghost films on television she curled up with her blanket and her teddy bear and watched until someone remembered she was there.

For the past few weeks no one had remembered very often. Her parents and her bigger brothers and sisters were too busy in the kitchen looking at paint colours and materials and drawing plans of their new rooms to notice what Amaranthus was doing. Which is why when the Najdorf family moved into the oldest house in the neighbourhood only Amaranthus knew it was haunted.

She knew as soon as she saw it. She could tell by the iron gate hanging off its hinges, the cracked tile path with weeds growing through, and the shroud of ivy that had wrapped itself round the house.

Inside the house the stairs creaked. There were soft scrabblings behind the walls. When she walked through the house there were footsteps behind her.

'Just echoes,' her father said. 'When the house is fixed up it'll be all right.'

But Amaranthus knew better.

The day they moved in, her bigger brothers and sisters chose a room at the top of the stairs for her. 'This is a nice room for you, Amaranthus,' they said. 'It's big and it's light and it couldn't possibly be haunted.'

'We'll see,' said Amaranthus.

Her big sister Maureen made up a mattress on the floor for her because the beds hadn't arrived yet, and put a basin under a damp patch on the ceiling. 'You'll be all right in here, won't you?' she said.

'I hope so,' said Amaranthus. She unpacked her pyjamas and her torch and her favourite puzzle book and got into bed to wait.

At first the only sounds were the wind sighing in the mango tree and the ivy tapping on the window panes. Amaranthus was just dropping off to sleep when there was a flash and a crash of thunder, and a sudden wind blew the windows open.

Amaranthus got up and shut the windows again; and in that moment there was a stealthy footfall behind her and the creak of an opening door. She looked round. In the flicker of the lightning she could see someone standing there.

It was her sister Maureen. 'Are you all right?' said Maureen. 'I thought you might want me to get into bed with you.'

'All right, then,' said Amaranthus, and moved over.

The next morning Amaranthus went looking for the ghost. She knew from all the films she had seen that the ghost usually lives in a small room at the end of a passage, and Amaranthus thought she had found the right place.

'That's going to be my work room,' said her mother when Amaranthus told her.

'I wouldn't bet on it,' said Amaranthus. She hummed a tune while
148   she waited for her mother to go away.

The work room was dark and draped with cobwebs, and Amaranthus did not see the ghost at first. Then something by the window caught her eye, and there he was, sitting hunched up on a pile of boxes with his chin resting on his knees, staring out of the window. She could tell he was a ghost by the way the light shone through him.

The ghost did not look at her, but after a few moments he hunched his shoulders a bit more and sank his head down on his chest and sighed.

'That was pretty good haunting last night,' said Amaranthus. 'I mean, with the lightning and everything.'

'Go away,' sighed the ghost, and his voice was like the wind in the mango tree.

'My name's Amaranthus, and I'm the youngest in the family.'

'Go away, Amaranthus,' whispered the ghost.

It was then that Amaranthus noticed how badly he was dressed. His trousers were held up with string, his jacket was too big for him and held together with bits of wire instead of buttons, and he wore his shapeless old boots without laces or even socks.

'Maybe we could tidy you up a bit first,' said Amaranthus. 'Hang on. I'll get you something.' She ran upstairs to where her parents were unpacking and said, 'Dad, have you got any old clothes?'

'I'm wearing them,' said her father.

'I mean for the ghost. His own clothes look awful.'

'Ah, dressing-up time, is it?' asked her father, and gave her a cardboard box full of old clothes.

'I think I prefer my own rags,' said the ghost when he saw them, and Amaranthus had to admit that the clothes she had brought him were not very much better. Her mother had cut all the buttons off them. 'Still, they may come in handy for something,' he said, fingering a pair of red woollen socks. Then he looked up at Amaranthus and said, 'Thank you. You can go now.'

Amaranthus didn't move. She wanted to see him put the socks on.

'Go. Go,' said the ghost, waving her away with his hand; and when she still didn't go he muttered, 'Oh, stay there, then,' and a moment later he had disappeared.

149

Amaranthus spent the rest of the day looking for him, but without success.

Next day she looked in the work room. Her mother was in there cleaning cobwebs off the window, and there was no sign of the ghost. Amaranthus searched the rest of the house, looking through all the dark corners and cupboards a ghost might hide in, before she thought of looking in the garden shed.

At first the shed looked empty, but then she saw a green glow in the far corner, and there was the ghost, sitting with his back to her. He was trying on the red socks.

'There you are,' said Amaranthus.

The ghost jumped round. 'Is nowhere private? Must you follow me everywhere I go?'

Now that he was facing her, Amaranthus saw that he had put on one of her father's shirts as well. Because it had no buttons, he had knotted the ends at his waist; it gave him a rakish air, like a pirate. 'You look nice,' she told him, then regretted it when she saw how embarrassed he was.

'I'm not used to being complimented,' the ghost said, winding his fingers together. A moment later he started to go fuzzy at the edges, but this time Amaranthus grabbed his shirt. Being real, it offered something to hold him by.

'Please don't go.'

'My dear young lady,' said the ghost, twisting away as far as he could and flapping at her with his insubstantial hands, 'you are offending the natural order of things. It is ghosts who are supposed to haunt, not little girls. Little girls should be seen and not heard.'

'I wasn't haunting you,' said Amaranthus. 'I just wanted to know your name.'

'I'm not sure I remember,' said the ghost. 'I think it's something like Parbury. But who cares?'

'I do. I like ghosts.'

'Nobody likes ghosts,' said Parbury. 'After you're dead no one cares about you any more. They fill your little room with sewing machines and filing cabinets and dressmakers' dummies, and they fill

151

your shed with mowers and lawn rakes, and they pack up all your special things, all your little bits and pieces, and sell them or take them to the tip.'

Parbury looked so unhappy while he said this that Amaranthus forgot and let go of his shirt for a moment; she knew her father had taken several boxes to the tip that morning. She was about to pat Parbury's arm in sympathy when she realised it had disappeared. The rest of Parbury had disappeared, too.

Later that morning a van arrived with the heavy furniture, and Amaranthus forgot about Parbury while she helped the moving men, skipping and darting about between them to show them where things went.

'That big old cupboard goes in my room,' she told them, 'and so does that bed.'

'Wouldn't you like to see if your mother needs a hand?' asked the moving men.

Amaranthus went downstairs and saw that her mother had moved a sewing machine and a dressmaker's dummy into the work room. Parbury was nowhere to be seen.

She looked through the house for him, checking all the dark corners, and then she tried the shed again. Parbury was not there, but she tripped over the mower and a rake.

That night at dinner her father said, 'Still playing ghosts, Amaranthus?'

'That depends,' said Amaranthus.

'Please don't,' said Maureen. 'There's a thunderstorm coming.'

But there was no thunderstorm that night, only a cold, soaking rain. Amaranthus looked through the house and shed one last time before she went to bed, but the only sign of Parbury was the box of clothes left in the work room. She took it upstairs with her.

Just before she got into bed she checked the window to make sure it was properly shut, and saw a faint greenish glow in the mango tree. It was Parbury. He was sitting in the topmost fork, with his collar turned up and his jacket pulled over his head against the rain.

152   'What are you doing out there, Mr Parbury?' she said.

'Is there anywhere else?' asked Parbury. But he climbed in through the window when she held it open, and took the dry towel she offered him.

'Ghosts don't get wet,' he explained. 'It's just my clothes.' Then he saw the cardboard box and said, 'Ah, good. You brought my dry things.'

Amaranthus was about to put the box away in her cupboard when she saw Parbury staring. 'That's a fine cabinet,' he said. 'A very fine cabinet indeed.'

'It came from the secondhand shop,' said Amaranthus.

'I had a friend once lived in a cabinet,' said Parbury. 'He had a very happy existence.'

'Would you like to live in this one?' asked Amaranthus. 'You're very welcome, and I promise not to open it too often.'

Parbury thought for a moment, nodding to himself. He climbed into the cupboard and turned around in it, spreading his elbows as if trying it for size. 'It's very good.'

He stepped out again and picked up the box of clothes. 'Thank you,' he said. 'I'll take it.' Then he climbed back into the cupboard, shutting the door behind him.

He is probably still in there.

Eric C. Rolls

MISS STRAWBERRY'S PURSE

Miss Strawbery has a long fat purse
To keep her money in.
It is a rare and handsome purse
Made of crocodile skin.
It is crocodile skin without a doubt
For she did not take the crocodile out
And when she walks to town to shop
He follows behind her clop, clop-clop,
And opens his mouth and bellows aloud
And swishes his tail amongst the crowd.
Now and again there's an angry mutter
As a man is swept into the gutter.
When in a shop it is time to pay
Shopkeepers look at the brute in dismay
When Miss Strawberry says, 'Crocky, open wide,'
And, 'Shopman, your money is deep inside.
Just dodge the slashing of his paws
And reach beyond those ugly jaws;
But I warn you if you make him cough
He'll probably bite your arm right off.'
The shopkeeper usually says, 'No worry.

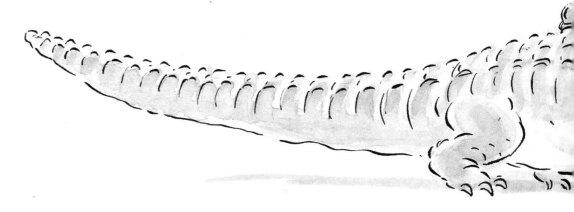

Pay next month. I'm in no hurry.'
But a grocer once, owed four-pounds-ten,
Said, 'That's worth more than one of my men.'
He called his errand-boy, 'Hey son,
Come over here, we'll have some fun.
I'll hold your legs and guard you while
You crawl in this quiet old crocodile
And collect in his vitals four-pounds-ten.
If you bring it out again
I'll give you sixpence for your trouble.
Come here, son, and at the double!'
Now the length of Miss Strawberry's crocodile's throat
Is four times as long as a shopkeeper's coat.
The crocodile opened fearfully wide
And the errand-boy crawled right down inside.
When he had gathered four-pounds-ten
And hurriedly tried to back out again,
The crocodile closed his jaws with a smile,
Saying, 'One of the joys of a crocodile,
Indeed you might say, his favourite joy,
Is making a meal of a messenger-boy.'

155

Barbara Giles

MARIA'S INVISIBLE CAT

MARIA thought a lot about having her own cat. Should she have a black cat, a tabby cat, a white cat?

'What colour cat do you like best, Dad?'

'I've told you not to ask for a cat,' said her mother.

'I'm not asking,' said Maria. 'What colour, Dad?'

'Black, I suppose. But Mum doesn't want a cat.'

'My cat is black, with a white tip to his tail,' said Maria. 'I can't think what to call him.'

'Call him Nix,' said Dad. 'That means "nothing". No-cat. Remember what Mum said.'

Maria liked the name. 'Nix is very little,' she said. 'Not much bigger than nothing. And he doesn't eat much.'

At kindergarten, Maria painted a black kitten with a white tip to his tail.

'His name's Nix,' she said to her teacher. 'Please write it for me.'

When her mother saw the painting she said, 'You can't have a cat.'

'I know,' said Maria, 'but please put up the picture for me.'

Her mother stuck it up on the wall with sticky tape.

After tea, Maria found an old saucer. 'Can I have this for Nixie?'

'There's no milk for No-cat,' said her mother.

'I know, I know,' said Maria. 'Can I have this box for his bed? Can I put it on the back veranda? Could he have this old jumper to sleep on?'

Her mother sighed.

Next morning, Maria opened the back door. 'Are you there, Nix? Come on, I've brought you some milk. Drink up, Nixie, so you'll grow big.'

'You're a silly,' said her mum. 'All that carry-on about a cat that isn't there! Now come and get ready for kindergarten.'

'Okay. Goodbye Nixie. I'll see you when I get home.'

When Dad came home that night she said, 'What *do* you think Nix was up to today? He was trying to get in the cat-door.'

'Don't you unfasten that door,' said Mum, 'or we'll have some stray in before you can sneeze. I meant it. No cats.'

'Okay,' said Maria. 'He likes it outside.'

Each day, Maria took food and milk out to Nix. At least, that's what she said, but the saucer was just as empty when she carried it out, very carefully so as not to spill any milk, as when she brought it back inside.

She shook out his bed and washed his saucer, and she talked to him a lot. She played with him, rolling a little pink ball. When nextdoor's dog got in, she said, 'Quickly, Nix. Up the plum tree. He can't get you there.'

She even took a photograph of him in the plum tree. 'You can't see him for the blossom,' she said, 'but there's the tip of his tail.'

After a while her parents got quite used to all this. Some nights her Dad would say, 'Have you fed your cat?' Or he'd ask where Nix was hiding himself.

Her mother said nothing, except that the empty box by the door looked untidy.

'He's no trouble at all, your little Nix,' said Dad. 'He doesn't scratch up the garden or chase the birds. Nobody would know we had a cat at all.'

'We *don't*,' said Mum. 'And that's the way it's going to stay. Maria's is quite the best kind of cat. Invisible.'

One night there was a storm which blew the rain right up to the back door. Maria brought the box inside.

'Nixie has to come in, or he'll get wet,' she said.

'Well, just this once,' said Dad with a wink.

Next day, the sun was shining after the rain, and Maria felt as if something good was going to happen.

During breakfast she heard a small sound outside, and she opened the door. On the mat was a small black kitten.

'Nix,' said Maria. 'Nixie. So here you are.'

The little cat miaowed softly.

'I didn't keep asking, did I?' said Maria. 'But he's come. I *can* keep him, can't I, Dad?'

'Perhaps he isn't here to stay. He may live somewhere nearby,' said her father. 'I don't know what Mum will say, but I'll talk to her.'

'See, here's his little white-tipped tail – just like I drew him,' said Maria. 'Are you hungry, Nixie?'

She filled his saucer with real milk, and Nixie lapped it up quickly.

'Look at his little pink tongue. And he's got a white patch on his back leg. I didn't know about that.' She stroked him. 'Nixie, Nixie, you *are* hungry. Nice puss. I'll fetch your box.'

The cat jumped into the box, purring, as if he belonged there. He was sleepy now. 'Will you tell Mum he's here, in his box, Dad? Tell her I won't let him inside. He'll be *almost* invisible. He will, really. *Please*, Dad.'

Later she heard her parents talking. Nothing was said about sending Nix away. No one came looking for a small black cat.

Each day Maria fed Nix on the back veranda. She washed his saucer and shook out the jumper from his box.

Nix was growing. He was quick and full of play. But he stayed outside. Mum ignored him when she came out. Nix was very quiet then, and crept into his box. He seemed to know she didn't like cats.

One Saturday morning, Maria and her father drove to the city to buy a special birthday present for Mum.

While they were out, Joe from next door raced in carrying Nix.

'Your little cat, Mrs Drew,' he said sadly. 'He's had an accident. Broken his leg, I'd say. Must have been hit by a car.'

'Poor little fellow,' said Maria's mum. 'We must get him to the vet quickly. But the car isn't here.'

'I'll take you,' said Joe.

So they went to the vet in Joe's big red truck.

The vet soon had Nix's broken leg in plaster. 'He is all right, but for the leg,' he said. 'Keep him quiet if you can.'

When they got home, Mrs Drew made a bed for Nix in her old Chinese sewing basket, and put it on the veranda. Nix lay quietly and stared up at her with his green eyes.

She went into the house.

Then she came out again.

'It's a bit cold out here for a hurt cat,' she said, and she carried the basket into the kitchen, and put it down near Maria's cat painting.

She sat down on the floor beside Nix and stroked his head.

'You're a good little cat, Nixie,' she said. 'How could I send you away?'

She was still sitting there, talking to Nix, when Maria and her father came home.

'He'll be all right,' she said, getting up quickly. 'Just a broken leg. Fetch him a saucer of milk, Maria. And unhook the cat door, so he can let himself in and out. He's a smart little cat, he'll soon understand how it works.'

'He's smart, but no longer invisible,' said Dad with a smile at Maria.

Nix drank a little milk, and tried walking on three legs. He was awkward at first, and timid, but soon he was sniffing his way round the kitchen as if he belonged there.

'This is home, Nix,' whispered Maria, 'and you're here to stay.'

'By the way, Maria,' said Mum. 'You could throw away that tatty box of his. He'll be much more comfortable in this basket.'

So it was lucky that Maria's birthday present for Mum was a special wooden box, with lots of compartments and tiny drawers with brass handles, to keep her sewing things in.

Kath Walker

CARPET SNAKE

HE was a beauty, that ten-foot carpet snake we had as a pet. My father belonged to the Noo-muccle tribe of Stradbroke Island, and the carpet snake was his totem. He made sure he looked after his blood-brother. My mother belonged to a different tribe. The carpet snake was not her totem. She hated old Carpie, because of his thieving ways. She was proud of her fowl-run and of the eggs our hens provided. Carpie liked the fowl-run too; every time he felt hungry he would sneak in, select the choicest fowl in the run, and swallow it. He could always outsmart Mother, no matter what she did to keep her chooks out of his ravenous belly. But, somehow, Mother never was game enough to bring down the axe on Carpie's head. We all knew she was often tempted to do just that. I think two things stopped her: her deep respect for the fact that Dad's decisions were final around the house, and the thought that if she killed in anger, Biami the Good Spirit would punish her.

We all loved Carpie, except for Mother – and the dog. The dog kept well out of Carpie's way, because he was scared stiff of him. He seemed to know that a ten-foot carpet snake can wind itself around a dog and, in time, swallow it whole.

Whenever Mother thought none of us kids was around, she would swear at old Carpie – and Mother's swearing could outmatch that of any bullocky anywhere in Australia.

One day Mother went away for a short while to hospital. She came home with a brand-new baby sister for us. The day of her home-coming, we were rather overawed as we watched the baby sleeping in

her cot. The big black dog looked at the baby, too, and obviously approved of the new arrival. After a while, Mother shooed us out to play, placed the cover gently over the sleeping baby, and went to make herself a cup of tea. Some friends, tribal neighbours, called to welcome her home. Playing in our summer-house of tea-tree bark that Dad had built to catch the cool breezes blowing from the bay, we heard the women gossiping and the clink of teacups. When the neighbours left, Mother peeped in with pride on her new baby.

Suddenly we heard Mother's voice raised in a terrible screech as she raced outside, calling to Dad. Dad read the urgency of that screech, dropped his hammer, and ran.

Mother looked as though she were having a fit. She was jumping up and down, running to snatch up the long-handled broom, swearing like a bullocky. We knew something terrible must have happened for Mother to carry on like this. She behaved differently in different sorts of emergencies. We knew this one was serious.

'Stop shouting, woman!' Dad ordered. 'What's wrong?'

Mother pointed a shaking finger towards the bedroom. 'Get that gluttonous reptile out of my bedroom!'

Dad went into the bedroom. There, curled up in the cot with the baby, now wide awake and crying, was old Carpie.

Carpie seemed to sum up the situation in no time flat. He quickly slithered off the bedclothes, down onto the floor and out of the door.

The dog was trying to do the right thing by the family, taking menacing steps towards the snake and making growling noises in his throat. He was very happy to obey Dad, however, when he called him off.

Finally Mother found her composure, once Carpie had disappeared. 'But you mark my words, you stubborn fellow, that snake could have swallowed my baby,' she told Dad.

'Don't be silly, woman, why would he want to swallow your baby when he can swallow your chooks any time he wants to?' Dad retorted, and shot out of the door before Mother could think up a reply.

164

After that old Carpie carried on exactly as before, roaming about the house wherever he pleased. He went on stealing fowls and eggs, and slept anywhere he liked – though he never again tried to get into my baby sister's cot. I used to like it when I went off to the lavatory and found him holed up there. He would stretch himself right out across a beam in the ceiling. I used to sit in the lavatory for hours and tell him my innermost secrets, and it was very satisfying the way old Carpie would never interrupt the conversation or crawl away. Mother often accused me of dodging chores by going off and spending such a long time in the lavatory. This wasn't quite true; all I wanted to do was to share my secrets with Carpie.

When Dad died, we lost Carpie. He just seemed to disappear. We never found out what happened to him. Perhaps Biami the Good Spirit whispered to him: 'Your blood-brother has gone to the shadow land. Your days are numbered. Get lost.'

I like to think he still roams somewhere. Maybe he found a better fowl-run. I hope so. Funny thing about Mother: when my father died and Carpie disappeared, she decided to give away her fowl-run. She seemed to lose interest in it, somehow.

Henry Lawson

TROUBLE ON THE SELECTION

You lazy boy, you're here at last,
  You must be wooden-legged;
Now, are you sure the gate is fast
  And all the sliprails pegged?
Are all the milkers at the yard,
  The calves all in the pen?
We don't want Poley's calf to suck
  His mother dry again.

And did you mend the broken rail
  And make it firm and neat?
I s'pose you want that brindle steer
  All night among the wheat!
If he should find the lucerne patch,
  He'll stuff his belly full,
And eat till he gets 'blown' on it
  And busts, like Ryan's bull.

Old Spot is lost? You'll drive me mad,
    You will, upon my soul!
She might be in the boggy swamps
    Or down a digger's hole.
You needn't talk, you never looked;
    You'd find her if you'd choose,
Instead of poking possum logs
    And hunting kangaroos.

How came your boots as wet as muck?
    You tried to drown the ants!
Why don't you take your bluchers off?
    Good Lord, he's tore his pants!
Your father's coming home tonight;
    You'll catch it hot, you'll see.
Now go and wash your filthy face
    And come and get your tea.

Ray Watts

SLANGUAGE

A swagman and a shearer met,
out on the sunshine track,
then stopped to see a settler,
who told them what they lacked:

'Yer teeth are like a dogleg fence,
you've white-ants in your billy,
as well you're both a shingle short,
stunned mullets aint as silly.'

Now the shearer he was touchy,
as a scrub-bull in a bog,
and the squatter landed on his back,
like a lizard on a log.

'Well, strike me handsome,
strike me fat,
stiffen all the snakes.'

'She's sweet son!'
the swaggie said,
'She's apples,'
said his mate,
then both of them
took to the scrub,
beside the station gate.

'Oh, starve the barber,
strike a light,
strike me up the gum trees;
starve the lizards,
stone the crows,
you're slow as a montha Sundies.'

Bill Scott

THE LIGHTHOUSE KEEPER
AND THE HERRING GULL

The lighthouse keeper sat on a rock and a sad, salt tear wept he.
'I'm tired of biscuits and tins of beef, I want a fish for tea!
But I haven't a hook and I haven't a line to throw in the salty sea.'

He peered to the east where the breakers broke, he blinked his teary eye.
He looked behind where his tower rose like a steeple in the sky
And he saw a wise old herring gull perched on a rock close by.

Said the keeper, 'A gull has an easy time when he wants a fish to swallow.
He rises up till he spies a shoal where the billows bellow hollow.
He dives down deep and he gulps a fish, with another one to follow.'

The keeper found a rusty nail and hammered it into a hook;
He ravelled a string both long and strong from his cosy sea-boot sock;
He baited the line and cast it in with a crafty, hungry look.

He caught a whiting and a bream, he almost caught a whale.
He hooked a crab by its big, round claws and a flathead by the tail,
And he tossed each fish behind him, where they fell in an old tin pail.

Then he snavelled a shark that broke his line. He didn't really care.
He had fish enough to fry for tea, and for breakfast, and to spare,
And even enough for the herring gull that he thought deserved a share.

So he turned around to view his catch with shouts of joy and mirth,
But his roar of rage at what he saw was heard from Cairns to Perth –
An empty pail, and the fullest, fattest herring gull on earth.

A.B. Paterson

MULGA BILL'S BICYCLE

'Twas Mulga Bill, from Eaglehawk, that caught the cycling craze;
He turned away the good old horse that served him many days;
He dressed himself in cycling clothes, resplendent to be seen;
He hurried off to town and bought a shining new machine;
And as he wheeled it through the door, with air of lordly pride,
The grinning shop assistant said, 'Excuse me, can you ride?'

'See here, young man,' said Mulga Bill, 'from Walgett to the sea,
From Conroy's Gap to Castlereagh, there's none can ride like me.
I'm good all round at everything, as everybody knows,
Although I'm not the one to talk – I hate a man that blows.

'But riding is my special gift, my chiefest, sole delight;
Just ask a wild duck can it swim, a wild cat can it fight.
There's nothing clothed in hair or hide, or built of flesh or steel,
There's nothing walks or jumps, or runs, on axle, hoof or wheel,
But what I'll sit, while hide will hold and girths and straps are tight;
I'll ride this here two-wheeled concern right straight away at sight.'

'Twas Mulga Bill, from Eaglehawk, that sought his own abode,
That perched above the Dead Man's Creek, beside the mountain road.
He turned the cycle down the hill and mounted for the fray,
But ere he'd gone a dozen yards it bolted clean away.
It left the track, and through the trees, just like a silver streak,
It whistled down the awful slope towards the Dead Man's Creek.

It shaved a stump by half an inch, it dodged a big white-box;
The very wallaroos in fright went scrambling up the rocks,
The wombats hiding in their caves dug deeper underground,
But Mulga Bill, as white as chalk, sat tight to every bound.
It struck a stone and gave a spring that cleared a fallen tree,
It raced beside a precipice as close as close could be;
And then, as Mulga Bill let out one last despairing shriek,
It made a leap of twenty feet into the Dead Man's Creek.

'Twas Mulga Bill, from Eaglehawk, that slowly swam ashore:
He said, 'I've had some narrer shaves and lively rides before;
I've rode a wild bull round a yard to win a five-pound bet,
But this was sure the derndest ride that I've encountered yet.
I'll give that two-wheeled outlaw best; it's shaken all my nerve
To feel it whistle through the air and plunge and buck and swerve,
It's safe at rest in Dead Man's Creek – we'll leave it lying still;
A horse's back is good enough henceforth for Mulga Bill.'

Bill Scott

MIRRUNGUN

THIS is a story from the mangrove tree country where the sea and land are all mixed up. That's where the trees wade in the water, fish run about on the mud and the little fiddler crabs wave their red claws at you from the banks.

Mirrungun came from that place. He was a bad man, always wanting to fight people. He had good weapons, his spears were sharp and he could throw them like a flick of lightning. You had to look out if he was fighting you! All the time he was laughing at people, making fun of them. The young men would get angry and try to fight him but he would always win, he was so clever and fast with his spears.

Too many young men were getting hurt. The old men talked about it. Then they went to Mirrungun and said, 'You'd better go away. You fight other men all the time about nothing. You are making trouble with our neighbours. You know we don't fight our neighbours unless they come here to our country when we haven't asked them to. That's the law. But you pick fights all the time. You'd better go away altogether until you learn to live at peace.'

Mirrungun was angry about what they said but he wasn't silly enough to argue with those old men in case they sent the killers after him. He said, 'All right. I'll go.'

Mirrungun had two wives. They were good women. They were sisters and didn't want to have to go away from their uncles and aunties and mother and father. Their hearts were sad, but a wife has to go with her husband. That's the law. Mirrungun said to them, 'Come on. These people don't want us to stay here. We have to go away now. They don't want us any more!'

The wives cried and wanted to stay. They said, 'If you stop fighting, we can stay.'

Mirrungun said, 'Come on, both of you, or I'll beat you,' so they all went. The old men went with them till they left the mangrove country to make sure Mirrungun didn't play a trick on them and come back.

They walked and walked, a long way. Afterwards they came to a hill, a place called Ngarun. There was a man lived there by himself, a clever man, a magician, very old and thin. His hair and beard were all white. His name was Ngarun too, the same as the place. It was his place; he was the boss of all that country around the hill.

Ngarun heard the women crying because they were sorry to leave their mother and father and all their relations. They were crying 'Neeeeeeeeee! Neeeeeeeeee! Neeeeeeeeeeeee!' as they walked along behind their husband. Old Ngarun came out of his camp and said to Mirrungun, 'What's the matter with these women? Why are they crying? Their faces are wet and their noses are running. How can I rest with all that noise going on? You shouldn't beat your wives unless they have been bad women, you know. That's the law. What did they do wrong?'

Mirrungun got angry because he hadn't beaten the women at all. He said, 'That's not your business, old man. If you don't like the noise you better go away. Leave us alone. I think I like this place. Maybe I'll stop here. Maybe we'll all stop here.'

He didn't really like the place, you know. It was all dry country, and he came from the salt-water country where the mangroves are. He was just wanting to fight.

Old Ngarun said, 'Hey! You can't do that! This is my place.'

'I can stay where I like,' said Mirrungun. 'You shut up or I'll spear you and take all this country for my own.' He wasn't really angry, he just wanted to fight, that's all.

Ngarun was a clever fellow, too clever for Mirrungun. He said, 'All right, you can stay. Come to my camp, I have a wallaby cooked. You can have some.' He pretended to be frightened but he wasn't.

Mirrungun and his wives went to the old man's camp and they all had some food to eat. It was getting dark. The old man said, 'You better go and make a fire for yourselves, it's getting dark.' Mirrungun just stretched out in the cool dust like a kangaroo and said, 'No. I like this place, you better go yourself. You can find another place.'

He was just making trouble. You can't put a man away from his own fire; that's the law. But the old man pretended to be frightened and said, 'It might be better if you go. This is my place and it only likes me to stay here.' But Mirrungun wouldn't go, he just lay there in the dust with his hand on his spear and wouldn't answer.

Ngarun bowed his head and went away from the fire, around the hill to his secret place where he kept all his magic things. He got them out from where they were hidden and lit a fire. Then he started to sing about Mirrungun, a great big magic song. Mirrungun didn't know, he had gone to sleep.

After a bit, something strange happened – Mirrungun broke in halves! There were two of him now, still the same but only half as big as before. He didn't wake up, and old Ngarun went on singing. Then Mirrungun broke again. There were four of him now, still smaller. Old Ngarun went on singing all night and Mirrungun kept breaking up into smaller and smaller pieces till by daylight there were lots and lots and lots of tiny Mirrunguns all over the place. They all had little wings now and could fly. Then the old man sang a magic wind that blew from the south and carried them all away, back to the mangrove country. Mirrungun was awake now but he couldn't do anything, he was too little.

Ngarun went back to his camp and talked to the two wives who were awake and wondering what had happened to their husband.

176

Ngarun said, 'He's gone now, you will have to get new husbands. I'll find some for you'. He got them new husbands from his own people. They were kind young men who looked after their new wives properly and cared for them so they didn't cry any more.

When some years had gone past and they had children, they took their families back to see their mother and father and relations in the north country, and they were so happy to see each other again that they all cried together.

Every Wet season Mirrungun comes south from the mangroves looking for his wives and their relations, and everybody else. He is still very angry. He carries his little spear and sticks it into everybody he meets. You probably call him a mosquito.

That Ngarun was a clever fellow, all right, but he made a lot of trouble for everybody, didn't he? Every time we hear that 'Neeeeeeeeeeee! Neeeeeeeeeeeeeee!' in the night we wish that old man had sent him right away altogether and not left him to stick his little spears into everybody.

Kath Walker

THE BUNYIP

You keep quiet now, little fella,
You want big-big Bunyip get you?
You look out, no good this place.
You see that waterhole over there?
He Gooboora, Silent Pool.
Suppose-it you go close up one time
Big fella woor, he wait there,
Big fella Bunyip sit down there,
In Silent Pool many bones down there.
He come up when it is dark,
He belong the big dark, that one.
Don't go away from camp fire, you,
Better you curl up in the gunya,
Go to sleep now, little fella,
Tonight he hungry, hear him roar,
He frighten us, the terrible woor,
He the secret thing, he Fear,
He something we don't know.
Go to sleep now, little fella,
Curl up with the yella dingo.

HOW FIRE CAME

A LONG time ago, the Aboriginal people didn't have any fire. They had to eat all their food raw because they couldn't cook it. In winter, when the icy wind blew and whitened the grass with frost, the people were cold and unhappy. They had long fur coats, but they still felt cold. On dark nights, the old men had to sit up, shivering, and sing magic songs because there was no fire to frighten away the bad things.

One man of this people was named Gooda. He was clever, but he was also selfish and mean. He was out hunting by himself one day when a big thunderstorm came. Gooda hid from the storm in a hollow tree, which was silly because the old tree was struck by lightning and set on fire. When he stopped feeling frightened, Gooda felt the warm air from the fire on his wet, cold skin, and he thought, 'What a wonderful new thing this is. It feeds on the dead wood like the kangaroos feed on the grass. I like this thing that keeps me warm. I think I'll just keep it!'

The other people noticed that Gooda went off to camp by himself every night after that. Sometimes they smelt delicious smoke from cooking meat that made their mouths fill with sweet water. 'What's this? What's this good smell we've never smelt before?' they asked one another, but nobody knew. When they asked Gooda he just said, 'Oh, that's something that belongs to me.'

The old men were clever. You couldn't hide anything from them. They found out about everything. They discovered Gooda had fire. He was cooking his food, he was keeping himself warm, and he was able to sleep all night because the fire kept the bad things away from him.

The old men went to him and said, 'This is a good thing you've got. Give some to us, please; we'd like a bit of it. We can feed it on dead wood, too, and do all the things you are doing.'

Gooda said, 'No! This is mine. I found it and I'm going to keep it all for myself. You'd better not try to steal any, either. I've put a singing magic around the fire so no one can take any away.' So he wouldn't give them any of the fire, though they asked and asked.

The old men went away and talked about it. Gooda's magic kept them from taking a bit of the fire from all around it. Then one very clever old man said, 'I'll fix him. I just thought of a trick. You leave him to me.'

He sang a magic song and a great big whirlwind came spinning along, dancing the way they do and picking up bits of bark and dead leaves and tossing them high into the air. It went to Gooda's fire. It couldn't get through the magic spell around the sides of the fire but it went over the top. Then it dropped its tail into the fire and picked up

181

burning bits of wood and hot coals and carried them into the sky. It danced away across the land, dropping bits here and there so little fires sprang up all over the place, and all the families were able to get some.

The people were happy then because they didn't have to shiver in the cold any more. They could cook their food instead of having to eat it raw. Best of all, the bad things stayed away at night, so the old men could sleep instead of having to stay awake and sing magic songs to protect everyone. People laughed at Gooda because the old men had tricked him. He got angry then, and went away.

But the old men knew that Gooda would try to get his own back. Every night they used to sit and talk about what they could do so he would not be able to take the fire away again.

At last the same very clever old man who had sung magic for the whirlwind said, 'Gooda is a rainmaker. That is his magic. Perhaps he will make a big flood of water and put all the fires out. I'll tell you what we can do. You know the little black bats that live in the dead trees? They're magic, you know. I'll turn us all into little black bats. They can catch spirit things, things nobody can see. When we are bats we'll be able to find the spirit part of the fire, the part that came from the lightning. We can hide it in our hollow trees. It won't matter then if all the fires go out; we'll still have some of the spirit.'

The others thought this was a good idea, so that's what they did. They turned into bats and hid the spirit of fire in the dead trees.

Gooda was sitting up on a mountain planning to hurt the people who had laughed at him. He was very angry. He sang magic songs to make clouds come in the sky and hide the sun. He kept singing and the clouds piled higher, going grey and then black. They seemed to cover the whole world. Then Gooda let all the rain go at once, like a waterfall. It put out all the fires in all the camps. Gooda laughed and shouted as loudly as thunder, he was so happy. When the rain stopped and he looked down from his mountain, there was no smoke anywhere in all the land.

That night, a dry wind came from the desert and all the water was dried up. Gooda slept on his mountain, but when he looked out the

183

next morning he could see little coils of smoke rising from everywhere. The people had got their fire back.

This was what happened.

When the land dried, the old men turned themselves back into people again and said, 'Take a piece of soft, dead wood from a dead tree and put it on the ground. Then take a thin, round bit of hard wood and spin and spin it fast into the soft wood. See, it gets hot! It starts to smoke! Now it catches the dried grass we have ready! The spirit of fire is in the dead wood now. It doesn't matter if the fires go out, we can always start them again!'

Gooda was so angry that he went away, and no one ever saw him again. From then on the people could cook food when they wanted, and be warm at night, and sleep well, safe from the bad things that creep in the dark bush and fly on the night winds.

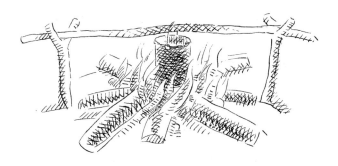

Geoffrey Dutton

NIGHT BIRDS

I wonder why
Birds sing by day, but at night they cry.

The curlews wail
As if they hope to find, but fail.

Oyster-catchers echo
Each other as if the beach were hollow.

The mopoke calls
How far away the darkness falls.

The rainbird spills
Notes into a dam that never fills.

Only the magpie
By moonlight sings and does not cry.

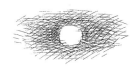

Pixie O'Harris

THE HUNTER

Slink back to your lair, brown fox,
There is danger for you in the sun,
Through the stringybark, black oak and box
The hunter is out with his gun.

The trout, lying still in the stream,
The water rat, gliding by roots,
The platypus, curled in a dream –
They will start when the fox hunter shoots.

Fly away, hungry crow, from the dam,
Old lizard, run under the rocks;
Keep close to your mother, young lamb
The hunter is out for the fox.

Jenifer Kelly Flood

IF YOU GO SOFTLY

If you go softly out to the gum trees
At night, after the darkness falls,
If you go softly and call –
   Tch, Tch, Tch,
   Tch, Tch, Tch,
   They'll come –
   the possums!

If you take bread that you've saved
They'll come close up, and stand
And eat right from your hand –
   Softly,
   Snatching,
   Nervous –
   the possums!

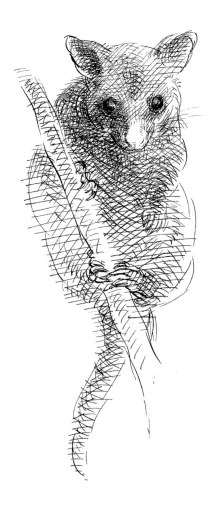

And if you are still, and move slowly,
You can, very softly, pat
Their thick fur, gently, like that –
    Its true!
    You can
    Really touch them –
    the possums!

You can do that all –
If you go softly,
At night,
To the gum trees,
If you go softly
– and call.

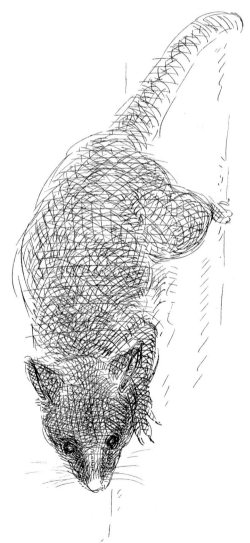

Jenny Wagner

JOHN BROWN, ROSE
AND THE MIDNIGHT CAT

ROSE'S husband died a long time ago.

Now she lived with her dog. His name was John Brown.

John Brown loved Rose, and he looked after her in every way he could. In summer he sat under the pear tree with her. In winter he watched as she dozed by the fire. All year round he kept her company.

'We are all right, John Brown,' said Rose. 'Just the two of us, you and me.'

One night, Rose looked out of the window and saw something move in the garden. 'What's that in the garden, John Brown?' she said.

John Brown would not look.

'Out there,' said Rose. 'I think it's a cat.'

'I don't see any cat,' said John Brown.

'I'm sure it's a cat. Go and give it some milk.'

'There's nobody there,' said John Brown.

But that night, when Rose was safe in bed, John Brown went outside. He drew a line all round the house and told the midnight cat to stay away. 'We don't need you, cat,' he said. 'We're all right, Rose and I.'

The next night Rose saw the midnight cat as he slipped through the shadow of the pear tree. 'Look, there he is, John Brown,' she said. 'Don't you see him now?'

But John Brown shut his eyes.

Rose sighed and packed up her knitting. Then she wound up the clock and took the milk bottles out.

John Brown followed her. 'I'm sure there's no cat,' he said.

But Rose saw the midnight cat often after that. Every night, when John Brown was not looking, she put out a bowl of milk.

And every night, when Rose was not looking, John Brown tipped it out again. 'You don't need a cat,' he said. 'You've got me.'

One night the midnight cat jumped up at the window and rubbed his back against the glass. His eyes were like lamps, and his fur shone against the ragged sky.

'Look, John Brown!' said Rose. 'Isn't he beautiful? Get up and let him in.'

'No!' said John Brown, and pulled the curtains shut. 'No, I won't let him in.'

Next morning Rose did not get up. John Brown waited in the kitchen for his breakfast, and nothing happened. He went to see what was wrong.

'I'm sick,' said Rose. 'I'm staying in bed.'

'All day?' said John Brown.

'All day and for ever,' said Rose.

John Brown thought. He thought all through lunchtime and when suppertime came, he was still thinking.

An hour past suppertime he went back to Rose, and woke her gently. 'Will the midnight cat make you better?' he asked.

'Oh, yes!' said Rose. 'That's just what I want.'

John Brown went out to the kitchen and opened the door, and the midnight cat came in.

Then Rose got up and sat by the fire, for a while. And the midnight cat sat on the arm of the chair . . . and purred.

THE WOMAN OF THE VOE

THERE was a fisherman of Unst.

This is in Zetland – or Shetland, as the English call it – where the folk live mostly by fishing. A land of ragged rocks and isles, it is, alone in the cold wild sea. Beyond the curve of the earth, lies Scotland. To the North, out of sight, are the Faeroe Isles, and as far beyond again is Iceland, with its strange fires and rivers of blue ice. And the folk of Unst know that a faerie race lived here in Zetland, and still does, from long before the coming of the Norsemen.

Now this fisherman's name is forgotten, but I think he was Jamie, one of the Black Jamies that later went away to the Highlands of Rosshire.

This Jamie the Black came down to the sea, alone, when both sun and moon shone at Midsummer. He should not have come then, for he surprised a company of Sea People who were dancing on the Voe.

You will know, perhaps, that these are of the Selkie folk, who in the sea wear sealskins, and dive to their deep caverns where there is air to breathe, and storms do not come, and they live in peace. It is the sun and moon of a summer's eve that bring them ashore, to put off their sealskins and dance together on the Voe.

193

When Jamie came over the lea, the Sea People took up their seal-skins and plunged into the foam and were gone. But Jamie had snatched up a skin that was at his feet, and away he went with it into the heather, and hid it deep among stones and fern.

When he came back from hiding it, a beautiful young woman was crying and searching, all alone on the Voe, and with her a small white dog, with red ears. Jamie knew, by this colouring, that it was a faerie dog. It came running to Jamie, showing its teeth, snarling and barking, threatening and savage. But the woman wept great tears, and begged him, 'Oh Jamie the Black, give me back my pelt! Give it me back, then!'

He'd have done it, for sure, but he'd fallen in love with her. It was a faerie spell that lay about her, and he'd stepped in it, and could not help himself.

'Voe Woman, marry me,' says Jamie.

But all she'd do was cry and beg him, and soon the little dog put his head against her and cried, too. Jamie was not a hard man. He almost gave in, but the spell of the love was so strong on him!

'Voe Woman, I promise to be good to you, and to your dog,' says Jamie. 'How can I let you go, when you've put a strong spell of love on me?'

No more could the woman help it that the spell lived about her. So at last she gave in, and said she'd marry him. Her dog, too, followed quietly to his cottage. But both woman and dog had a beaten look, and hung their heads, so that Jamie's heart near broke to see them. At that time the Black Jamies were not hard men.

'I'll love you best of any,' he promised her, 'and your dog will never hear the harsh word, should he chase the sheep or whatever.'

So she married him, did the woman of the Voe.

She had a fine boy child, and then a bonny girl. The little white dog guarded them well.

But often, when Jamie was away fishing, she'd go down to the Voe, and a big dog seal would come to her, from the North, and they'd talk together in a strange language.

She was neighbourly enough with the other fishwives, but she never spoke much. Always there was a sadness about her. Her eyes, green they were, would ever look far and away, as though she were listening to music that folk of the shore could not hear. Her dog, too, never left her side, save to be with the children at their play. Other fishwives

talked of her, wondering what was the spell she cast; for they felt it near her, in a turn of her head, a lift of her arm.

One day, when the children were searching for shells and sea pods along the shore, the little dog chased a pheasant into the heather. The children ran after, merry for them (for they were wistful children, though bonny). Now the little dog scampered and the children made happy cries like birds on the wing, and all of them ran into the heather.

The pheasant scent led the little dog to a place of stones and fern, and here he scratched and whimpered and barked with all his might. The children came up, and the boy tumbled a stone. The girl said, 'Mind your toe, wee Jamie!' and then she tumbled another.

'Here's a thing, wee Shona,' said the boy to his sister, and began to pull at something. In a minute they looked and it was an old sealskin. The little dog cried and scratched and the children pulled. At last they dragged it out – crumpled and rain-worn, but all of a piece, it was.

Their mother was slowly following, along the sudsy tide line where waves broke on the shore.

'See what we've found, Mam!' they called to her, as they came running. Was not the little dog all alive with wags, then! Did ever a small dog's tail go! He jumped and barked shrill, out of himself with the excitement.

The Voe Woman took the sealskin from them. Great tears ran down her face, and she carried it to the Voe. She called a long, long cry, with all the sadness of the sea in it; it was a cry, deep and green. Something came above the waves, and it was the sleek head of the great dog seal. Calling and crying, he came close to the Voe, while the woman put on, once more, her pelt.

Just then, Jamie's boat returned from the sea. From afar, he heard the strange cry of his wife, and the answering cry of the dog seal, and the barking of the small white dog on the shore. He beached his boat and ran along the shingle, and tears fell from his eyes.

'You'll not be leaving us all?' he cried to his sea woman.

But well he knew that now she had her sealskin back there was nothing he could do to keep her. The spell was broken. He'd no power to bid her stay, for her blood was of the salt seas and her heart of briny foam, and deep must call to deep.

She turned back to him and kissed him, and her bairns she kissed right well. 'You were a good man, then,' she told him. 'My bairns are right bonny, too. But I always loved my first husband best. I canna live with a grieving heart.'

So, leaving them, she followed the great dog seal, and the small white dog went with them. He ran back again and again to the children, trying to pull them to the sea. But when they could not come, he gave a long howl, and followed the two black seal heads, far down beneath the waves.

Sure, Jamie of the Voe married another fishwife, and she cared well for his children. But, from that day, the Black Jamies were dour men; and they walked no more on the Voe at Midsummer.

Jenny Wagner

THE WEREWOLF KNIGHT

EOLF was a knight and a good friend of the king, but at other times he was a werewolf. That is to say, when the moon rose over the tops of the pine trees, Sir Feolf took off his fine woollen tunic and his cloak, hid them under a big rock, and turned into a wolf. All night long he would run in the forest, and when morning came he would change into a man again, get dressed and go home, and no one was any the wiser.

Now a werewolf is a horrible beast to see, with his long fangs and his red tongue and his smoking breath, and Feolf was careful that no one ever saw him in this state; for even as a wolf his heart was kind, and he did not want to frighten anyone.

And so it was that the Lady Fioran, who was Feolf's dearest friend, walked with him in the garden, and sat with him at dinner, and never once suspected there was anything amiss.

Fioran was the daughter of the king, and loved Feolf even more than her father did. When the king saw this he was greatly pleased, for Feolf and Fioran were the two he loved best in all the world. And when Feolf and Fioran decided to get married, the king was overjoyed.

The king called for a feast that night, to mark the great event. The

198

cups were filled with mead, the lords and ladies chattered, and the minstrels sang of great deeds long ago.

But before their song was ended, the moon rose. And Feolf slipped away to the forest and turned into a wolf.

He did not come back till morning, and then Fioran found him walking in the garden. 'Where have you been, Feolf?' she asked.

But Feolf would not answer.

Then Fioran began to weep, for she was afraid he no longer loved her; and when Feolf saw this he was sorry, and told her his secret.

Fioran was deeply troubled. She loved the knight very much, but it is a different thing to be married to a werewolf, and to tell the truth she was very much afraid. She imagined the wolf, with his gleaming eyes and his cruel teeth and his lolling tongue, and she dreaded marrying such a horrible beast.

And so she puzzled and grew more sad, and the wedding day drew closer and closer.

On the eve of her wedding day she went to the court magician and asked him what she should do.

'The answer is simple,' said the magician, who would have liked to marry Fioran himself. 'When Sir Feolf goes to the forest tonight he will hide his clothes under a rock. You must bring back his clothes and give them to me.

'Is that all?' said Fioran. 'Just bring back his clothes?'

'Then all will be well,' said the magician.

That night, when Feolf slipped away to the forest, Fioran followed him. She brought back his clothes just as she was told and gave them to the magician.

When Feolf saw that his clothes were gone he pawed the ground and searched, and snuffed, and howled most piteously. 'Fioran!' he cried. 'Fioran!'

But a wolf does not have the gift of human speech, and only the crows in the pine trees heard him, and flapped their wings.

And so it was that Feolf did not come back to the castle that morning. For without his clothes he could not change back into human form, but must stay for ever a wolf.

Far away in the castle, on her wedding day, Fioran waited. She put on her wedding dress and twined flowers in her hair, but Feolf did not come.

In the evening she went to the court magician. 'Where is he?' she asked. 'What has happened to him?'

'He was a werewolf,' said the magician. 'You are better off without him.'

Then Fioran shut herself in her room and wept for her lost knight, and no one could comfort her; not the ladies of the court, nor the jesters, and not even the court magician, who kept sending her little presents.

The king was deeply saddened at the loss of his favorite knight, and decreed a time of mourning. There was no more feasting and no more dancing, and the minstrels hung their lutes on the wall.

Summer passed and autumn came, and Feolf stayed in the forest, living on wild roots and pine needles. The days grew colder and darker, and Feolf longed to be in the castle once again. He missed the feasting and the dancing, and he missed the warmth of his feather bed. But he missed Fioran most of all.

The king's sorrow grew as winter came, and one day his courtiers, trying to distract him, persuaded him to go hunting with them in the forest. 'We might kill a bear,' they said. 'Or a wolf.'

And so one icy day the king rode out with his huntsmen and his hounds. Feolf heard the hunting horns from far off and laughed for joy, for he knew the king was coming; and he ran to meet his master, loping his wolfish lope and grinning his wolfish grin.

The huntsmen saw the wolf as he came on them in the clearing, but they did not know it was Feolf. They saw the horrible beast with his dripping jaws and his glittering eyes, and the nearest huntsman aimed his spear.

'Stop!' cried the king. 'Drop your spear!'

The huntsman dropped his spear, but he kept his eye on the wolf. 'Take care, sire,' he said. 'A wolf is a savage beast, and should be killed before it does harm.'

But the king looked long at Feolf, and said, 'He is a sad wolf, and I cannot find it in my heart to kill him. Take him back to the castle and give him food and find him a warm place to sleep.'

The huntsmen thought the king's long grief had turned his mind, and some would have killed the wolf then and there if they had not feared the king's anger. But they tied a rope round Feolf's neck, keeping well clear of his jaws, and started off for the castle.

When they drew near the castle Feolf lifted his head and sniffed; and then he bayed and howled with joy.

Fioran in her bedchamber heard it, and came running out in her dressing gown, and ran to meet him and kissed him, and held his shaggy head between her hands and wept. Those who saw it were amazed, and all agreed that he was a very gentle wolf, even a noble wolf, but no one could tell the reason.

Fioran called the court magician and told him to bring Feolf's clothes. And before the astonished court Feolf put his clothes on and stood there once more as a noble knight.

202

The king was overjoyed to see Feolf again, the more so because Feolf had been loyal to him twice over; for even as a wolf he had been true to his king.

Then the king caused a feast to be set in the great hall, with dancing and merriment. The lutes were tuned again, the minstrels smoothed their throats with ale, and the ladies got out their dancing shoes.

Feolf and Fioran led the dancing that night, and when the moon rose Feolf did not go to the forest, but stayed with his bride. He had had enough of running wild in the forest, and from now on he was content to be just a man.

Only sometimes, when the night was particularly cold or the moon particularly bright, Feolf would slip away to the forest. But then Fioran kept a spare set of clothes for him, just in case.

Judith Wright

FULL MOON RHYME

There's a hare in the moon tonight,
crouching alone in the bright
buttercup field of the moon;
and all the dogs in the world
howl at the hare in the moon.

'I chased that hare to the sky,'
the hungry dogs all cry.
'The hare jumped into the moon
and left me here in the cold.
I chased that hare to the moon.'

'Come down again, wild hare.
We can see you there,'
the dogs all howl to the moon.
'Come down again to the world,
you mad black hare in the moon,

'or we will grow wings and fly
up to the star-grassed sky
to hunt you out of the moon,'
the hungry dogs of the world
howl at the hare in the moon.

Acknowledgements

The Publisher and Editors are grateful to the following for permission to reproduce copyright material in this publication:

Angus & Robertson Publishers for 'The ant explorer' from *A book for kids* by C. J. Dennis, © the publisher 1949; for 'The penguin bold' and 'Tale of a despicable puddin' thief' from *The Magic Pudding* by Norman Lindsay, © Janet Glad 1970; for 'Mulga Bill's bicycle' and 'Old Man Platypus' from *The collected verse of A. B. Paterson* and *The animals Noah forgot* by A. B. Paterson, © Retusa Pty Ltd; for 'Carpet snake' from *Stradbroke Dreamtime* by Kath Walker, © Kath Walker 1972; for 'Full moon rhyme' from *Collected poems 1942–1970* by Judith Wright, © Judith Wright 1971.

Jacaranda Wiley Ltd for 'The bunyip' from *My people* by Kath Walker.

J M Dent & Sons Ltd for 'Frightening the monster in Wizard's Hole' from *Nonstop nonsense*, and for 'A witch poem' and 'When the king rides by' from *The first Margaret Mahy story book* by Margaret Mahy.

John Johnson (Authors' Agents) Ltd for 'Pussycat, pussycat', 'When Old Mother Hubbard' and 'Country lunch' from *Wry rhymes for troublesome times* (Kestrel 1983, © Max Fatchen 1983), and 'If you hold a shell to your ear' from *Songs for my dog and other people* (Kestrel 1980, © Max Fatchen 1980) by Max Fatchen.

Oxford University Press, Australia, for 'The ears of Mandy' by June Epstein and 'John's task' by Mary Roberts from *Big Dipper*; and for 'Sinabouda Lily' from the picture-book of that name by Robin Anderson.

Penguin Books Australia Ltd for 'Brenda Baker' from *In the garden of bad things* by Doug MacLeod; and for 'John Brown, Rose and the midnight cat' from the picture-book of that name by Jenny Wagner.

Rigby Education for 'When I went to Byaduk' from *Songs for my thongs* by Colin Thiele.

Spike Milligan Productions Ltd for 'Three soldiers' by Spike Milligan.

All items not listed here are reproduced by kind permission of the authors.

Every reasonable effort has been made to contact and acknowledge correctly the owners of copyright material reproduced in this book.